D1538565

DESTINY CALLS

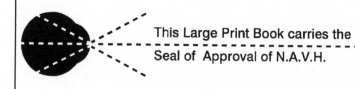

This Large Print Book carries the
Seal of Approval of N.A.V.H.

DESTINY CALLS

LINDA HUDSON-SMITH

THORNDIKE PRESS

A part of Gale, Cengage Learning

GALE
CENGAGE Learning

Detroit • New York • San Francisco • New Haven, Conn • Waterville, Maine • London

GALE
CENGAGE Learning

Copyright © 2009 by Linda Hudson-Smith.
Thorndike Press, a part of Gale, Cengage Learning.

Thorndike Press® Large Print African-American.
The text of this Large Print edition is unabridged.
Other aspects of the book may vary from the original edition.
Set in 16 pt. Plantin.
Printed on permanent paper.

LIBRARY OF CONGRESS CATALOGING-IN-PUBLICATION DATA

Hudson-Smith, Linda.
    Destiny calls / by Linda Hudson-Smith. — Large print ed.
        p. cm. — (Thorndike Press large print African-American)
    ISBN-13: 978-1-4104-2414-3 (alk. paper)
    ISBN-10: 1-4104-2414-6 (alk. paper)
        1. African Americans—Fiction. 2. College teachers—United States—Fiction. 3. Large type books. I. Title.
PS3608.U3495D47 2010
813'.6—dc22   2009047186

Published in 2010 by arrangement with Harlequin Books S.A.

Printed in the United States of America
1 2 3 4 5 6 7 14 13 12 11 10

This novel is dedicated to
the loving memory of
BELINDA JO SMITH
Your memory will live on forever
in the hearts of your beloved family
Sunrise: October 11, 1962
Sunset: November 13, 2008

Dear Reader,

I sincerely hope you enjoy reading *Destiny Calls.* I had so much fun with Dakota Faraday, a dynamic young woman with some closely guarded secrets, and Ethan Robinson, a fascinating English professor who discovers one of these secrets, only to learn much, much more.

I'm very interested in hearing your comments and thoughts on my story. If you would like to receive a reply, please enclose a self-addressed, stamped envelope along with all your comments to: Linda Hudson-Smith, 16516 El Camino Real, Box 174, Houston, TX 77062. Or you can e-mail your comments to lindahudsonsmith @yahoo.com. Please visit my Web site and sign my guest book at www.lindahudson smith.com.

Linda Hudson-Smith

PROLOGUE

"How do you like it?" Persia asked the caller, her tone soft and seductive.

"Slow, wet and hot," the bass voice responded. "I like to take my time."

"Interesting. I believe slow and easy is always better. I go for lots of foreplay. That's what makes me wet. What's your favorite position?" she asked, trying not to cringe. No matter how many men she talked to, she still had a hard time voicing certain lines.

"Are you always open to what the man wants?"

"Definitely. I'm a girl who likes to please her man, but I have limitations."

"Everyone is entitled to restrictions. How often do you like to have sex?"

"Whenever the mood hits me. It's not always possible to follow through, especially at inopportune times."

"I like the woman on top. What do

you prefer?"

"I love the man to be in control, but I don't have a problem swapping roles."

"I think I know what you mean," he responded. "Do you ever resort to self-pleasuring? I love women who are into that. There's something strong about them."

Persia stuck her finger down her throat in a mock gesture of gagging herself. Even if she was into it, she wouldn't share it with him. It was a healthy alternative, but just not for her. She quickly put herself in check. She had to work.

"I know the majority of men are into that, but I'm not sure if all women indulge. You guys start that at a really early age, but I understand it's healthy."

"I started at fourteen. My friends told me I was a late bloomer."

"But why would I ever do that when I've got you? I love how you give it to me. I can't imagine self-pleasuring would make me feel nearly as good as you do right now."

"You'd be surprised. Maybe you should try it. I can already visualize you in the act." He groaned with desire.

"Either way, this experience is utterly amazing. Visualize me taking you all the way there. I feel you inside of me," she said, sounding breathless. "Can you feel how hot

I am for you?" Persia knew she had the caller going. His breathing was way past labored.

"You feel hot enough to pop my thermometer. I love it when you get this hot and crazy with desire for me," he whispered sweetly.

She moaned softly, wantonly. "I love it when you whisper sweet things to me. Just for that, the candy store is open only for you. You can taste both the white and dark chocolates and lots of my other delectable sweets. What's your tongue's pleasure?"

At this point, Persia almost always changed gears, revving up her client's engine, taking hot and heavy to another level, making it hard for him to stay in control. As he cried out her name, she knew he was toppling. Persia screamed out simultaneously.

Persia could always tell what was going on with the client. His low guttural moans were a clear indication. A lot of times it didn't take very much to get the men off and running. As he continued gasping, Persia cringed inwardly, warding off tears. Never once had she fulfilled one of these calls without crying during or afterward.

He had simply referred to himself as Larry when he'd first come over the line. He'd also said he loved her name. It was exotic and sounded erotic to him. She had an idea this guy would become one of her regulars. He had sounded comfortable with her.

Persia let her mind wander as she waited for his breathing to return to normal.

She'd only taken on this job as a phone-sex operator, referred to as a PSO in adult entertainment industry (AEI) lingo, because it was excellent money, helping her work her way through college. There'd been no way around it. The demands on her salary were major.

The only requirements were that a PSO had to be eighteen and comfortable with scripted scenarios. Working from home required a corded landline phone. The beginning salary started from eight to twenty-five dollars an hour, depending on the time of day a PSO worked.

While online researching AEI Persia learned that fantasy phone sex generated between $750 million and $1 billion in revenues each year. As much as fifty percent of the money was retained by U.S. long-distance carriers.

"What do you do for a living?" Persia finally inquired.

The man sighed hard. "I work in medicine."

"What do you do in medicine?"

"I'm a physician, family practice."

This wasn't so unusual to Persia. She had many professionals calling her. Clients were given a special code number to punch in if they wanted to talk directly to a specific employee. She was rather surprised at the number of professional men who called her repeatedly. Many had asked her out, but it was against company policy. Besides, she refused to take the job home. This gig was taken out of pure necessity.

The job training had been terribly hard for her to get through. The dialogue often caused her to nearly gag. She didn't use a lot of the terminology from the different scripts, but she managed to get by without getting too graphic. She often thought about quitting, but it wasn't even an option for her. So much was involved here.

Persia's work area consisted of a multiline phone, a comfortable leather swivel chair, a semicomfortable cot and a small desk. Soft music was piped in 24/7. Many of the women had said they performed their jobs better when lying down on the twin-sized cot. Other employees preferred to sit on the leather swivel chair or even stretch out on the plush carpeted floor. There was also a television in the room.

If the women felt they needed assistance in their duties, there was plenty of X-rated material for them to view. Adult magazines were also plentiful. Some women worked at home, but Persia had chosen not to connect a phone line into her apartment.

A number of clean, well-stocked bathrooms were available for the employees. There were vending machines in the building, so when the ladies were munchy they could also eat and drink something. If they didn't want to exit the workplace, a refrigerator was available for those who chose to bring in their meals.

Persia worked four hours in the early evenings, going straight from school to the job, with another stop in between, but she was always home by dark. Only working three days a week allowed her flexibility with her other scheduled activities. Never did she work weekends, but Friday, Saturday and Sunday paid a much higher salary than what weekdays garnered. The call volume was extremely high during the weekends, referred to as prime time.

Because her client had paid for an hour, with half of it spent, the next thirty minutes Persia and Larry got back into some heavy sexual dialogue, but the heavier stuff came from him.

■ ■ ■ ■

The minute Persia disconnected the line, she stashed her alter ego.

Dakota Faraday ran for the area in the back of the building to punch out from the job paying way more money than she'd ever make in retail or fast food. Until something came along that covered all her expenses, she had to stay put. The desire to earn a degree had her trying desperately to look past how her needs were met. It was possible to land some other kind of job, but Persia already knew it wouldn't pay as much as she was making at Licensed to Thrill.

CHAPTER 1

In her bathroom, inside her Carson, California, apartment, decorated in various shades of baby blues and soft whites, Dakota Faraday peered into the looking glass, plucking away at her sable eyebrows. Every now and then she had to stand on her tiptoes to get in closer to the mirror. The lighting was bright enough, but she'd made a mess of her eyebrows a time or two, so she tried being more careful. Tweezing hurt, stung, but she didn't like waxing because it was even more painful. Shaving could result in razor bumps, so that hair-shaping method didn't work either.

Satisfied that she'd done a great job with her brows, Dakota reached into the glass shower cubicle and turned on the cold water full blast. People thought she was crazy for taking cold showers, but it was her preference. When taking a bath, she used steaming hot water and lots of bubbles and exotic oils. Baths were for relaxing. Showers were meant to invigorate. If she took a hot shower, she'd feel sleepy right afterward. Who wanted to feel that way when starting their day or going out on the town?

As the first douse of cold water ran over her ginger-brown flesh, she shivered and danced around a bit. Seconds later, she was all into it. Rarely did she stay in the shower longer than ten minutes at a time. Catching a cold was something she didn't want. Lying in wait for her outside the stall was the thick, white terry-cloth robe she'd slip into right after each bone-chilling experience. The towel warmer kept her fluffy bath sheet heated through and through, creating luxurious sensations against her body.

Dakota stepped out of the cubicle and quickly wrapped her body in the towel, glancing down at the dark granite counter where her watch lay. She was eager to check out the time. She had a hot date tonight and she wanted to be ready when Ethan showed up at her door. They'd been dating only a few weeks, seeing each other a few times a week. The couple was still in the getting-to-know-you stage, but she already thought he was a really great guy, gracious and gentlemanly.

Ethan Robinson was also drop-dead gorgeous, but Dakota hadn't once gotten the impression he was at all into himself. This fine brother had the darkest, sexiest eyes she'd ever seen, coal-black and piercing. Sometimes she felt like he could see straight through to her soul, although she hoped not.

As Dakota stood in front of the mirror once again, fully dried off now, she began to put on her special evening face. Carefully she applied a lightweight foundation and sealant powder and blush to her near-flawless ginger complexion. Streaked with warm bronze highlights, her silky sable hair hung down to her shoulders in thick waves.

A very light layer of eyeliner and a bit thicker one of mascara was administered next. Her hazel eyes, large and luminous, often gave away her deepest feelings despite her attempts to keep them hidden, especially from men.

Dakota saw a very pretty girl reflected in the mirror, petite in stature, yet well-built. In spite of her short legs, they were full, shapely and smooth as satin, possessing strong, well-defined calves, thanks to her daily twenty-minute workout.

Back in her master bedroom, where the decor was also blue and white, with frilly lace and satin, Dakota sat atop the queen, four-poster bed to lotion her legs and feet. She loved to go hoseless in the summer. Even though it was very early fall, she could still get away with bare legs, which had never felt more freedom. She also wore thigh-high stockings, but only on special dress-up occasions. They were comfortable and sexy.

Dakota got up from the mattress and smoothed back in place the blue and white lace and satin eyelet comforter, which perfectly complemented the white Provençal furniture. She had been extremely lucky in finding the bedroom set at a thrift shop, unable to believe how reasonably priced it had been. The headboard, dresser, chest of drawers and nightstands were in tiptop shape and didn't have visible marring anywhere. A lovely white desk and hutch completed her bedroom furnishings.

Slipping with ease into her slim off-white A-line skirt, she quickly zipped and buttoned the side closure. While pulling over her head a tangerine silk crepe shell, she was careful not to get makeup on it. She planned to take the matching sweater along on the date, as the nights in Los Angeles could turn pretty chilly, especially in the beach areas. Ethan had mentioned Redondo

Beach Pier as the dining venue.

The doorbell rang at the same time she slid her feet into tangerine patent leather pumps. She loved bright, flashy colors, which was evident in her limited but adequate wardrobe. There wasn't a lot of money in her budget to spend on clothes. Dakota loved to browse the consignment shops in upper-crust neighborhoods. It was like going on a treasure hunt. More often than not, she walked away with some pretty fabulous, excellent quality merchandise — and for very little money.

Grabbing her sweater off the bed, she ran for the door of her two-bedroom apartment. Dakota's heart rate instantly picked up speed. Ethan. His gentle touch did crazy things to her, producing alien yet pleasurable sensations.

As Dakota reached her compact living room, she looked around to see that everything was in place. The only furniture she owned for the living room was a nice sofa and matching chairs, done in a variety of earth tones. They, too, had come from secondhand establishments she frequented. The coffee and end tables, carved out of mahogany hardwoods, were newer than everything else. She had purchased them with her last income-tax check at a going-out-of-business sale, which meant she hadn't had to pay an arm and a leg to take ownership. The off-white and creamy beige area rug brightened the entire room. A couple of African-American works of art graced the ecru walls.

The bell pealed again before Dakota got there. She was so nervous. Her palms already felt sweaty. After peering into the small security window, she finally swung back the door wide, pulling off a beautiful, brilliant smile. "Hey, you, come on in."

Twenty-nine-year-old Ethan Robinson, tall and sexy, stepped inside. Dressed in beige Dockers and a deep lavender silk shirt, open at the collar, he looked delicious. As soon as his dark eyes connected with hers, he bent his head and landed a light kiss on her full mouth. His head was covered with loose golden-brown curls, which complemented his bronze, smooth complexion. He also had a dark mole just above the corner of his mouth, on the right side. She loved how it added to his sex appeal.

Smiling softly, he smoothed back an unruly strand of hair from her oval-shaped face. "I was thinking about you all day." His smile was broad and electric, nearly causing her knees to buckle. Ethan had straight white teeth and was proud to show them off.

He reached down and took her hand. "Are we ready?"

She nodded. "Got everything I need."

Removing the key ring from her hand, Ethan secured the apartment door.

As the couple began the short walk to his car, he gently dropped his arm around her shoulders. "There *are* advantages to living on the first floor of a three-story complex, especially when the elevator doesn't work. I always get my favorite spot right outside every time I've come over."

"You *have* been lucky. Tenants are assigned covered parking spots in well-lit areas nearby. I used to park in a visitors' slot until management caught on. I was reprimanded, of course."

Ethan placed a light kiss on Dakota's forehead. Just that slight touch set off a firestorm below his waistline. He fought hard to keep his manhood from responding, but he had been on fire for Dakota from day one. "Let's get a move on then."

Getting into the car wasn't a surefire way for Ethan to keep his visible desire in check, but it might help to hide it. Dakota wasn't ready for anything more than the few kisses and hugs they'd shared — and he wasn't the kind of man who'd press her. Any physical connection of the intimate kind had to come by mutual agreement. He found her exciting and refreshing, a far cry from some of the women he'd run into.

Learning that twenty-four-year-old Dakota was studying to become a teacher was a good feeling for him. She had said she'd gotten a late start on her educational goals, but she hadn't told him the reason. Once she received her B.S. and teaching certification, she planned a career in special education. He had a good friend who was in the same field. There were never enough educators and special-education teachers were badly needed.

Dakota smiled every time she saw the silver convertible. Equipped with a mesh wind protector, the top was already down. She didn't have to worry about her hair. She had a natural wave pattern and there wasn't much that could destroy it.

"Your car looks like it was recently washed and waxed, but I can't recall seeing it any other way. I guess if I had this nice of a ride I'd keep it spotless, too."

Opening the door for Dakota to get in, Ethan chuckled. "After our first date, I was sure I had bored you to tears by telling you how much I loved my brand-new car. Once

I got home, I realized I'd acted like a stupid teenager with his first set of wheels."

"You *did* talk about it a lot, but you weren't boring. Your enthusiasm was contagious and so were you. Cute, too."

"Cute, huh?" he mocked her, slipping into the driver's seat. He instantly started the engine and backed out carefully.

Dakota was comfortable on the plush ash-gray leather seat and her mind instantly reverted back to when and where they'd first met. It was one of her fondest memories. She touched his arm gently. "Do you remember our first meeting?"

"I'd never forget it. A few weeks have passed, but it's still fresh in my mind. The library near your junior college campus happens to be in my Torrance neighborhood."

"You mean your upper-crust hood, don't you?"

"That's how *you* see it. What do you remember about that day?"

"I was going to the library to pick up a couple of books to complete a research assignment. The fall term had just begun," Dakota remarked, thinking back on it.

Although Ethan worked as an assistant professor of English at a prestigious Southern California university, he'd gone to the Torrance Library to pick up a book he'd needed right away. Driving all the way back to the campus where he worked would've eaten up a lot of time.

Ethan briefly looked over at Dakota and smiled. "We reached for the same book at the same exact time. As our hands connected, we both felt the sizzle."

Dakota batted her lashes. "Before I could look away, you had me captivated."

"While you stood there blushing like a new bride on her wedding night, I took the initiative to introduce myself to you. It's one of the smartest things I've ever done."

He had told Dakota how desperately he had to have the book they'd both gone for.

" 'If you let me check it out first, I'll see to it that you know exactly when I plan to return it to the library,' " she teased, citing him verbatim. " 'I'll need a phone number to do that.' You were a smooth one, but I also got the impression you were sincere."

"Don't you know for sure yet?"

"The jury hasn't ruled on it, but it seems to me they're leaning in your favor."

"I was pleasantly surprised when you forked over your number."

Dakota grinned. "I did, didn't I? I was surprised, too."

Unable to get Dakota out of his mind, Ethan had ended up calling her the same evening. The couple had stayed on the line talking for a solid two-and-a-half hours, resulting in his asking her out on a first date.

Ethan held a Ph.D. in English Literature. Dakota recalled his telling her something about wanting to write a nonfiction book in the near future with a grant he hoped to receive, but he hadn't gone into much detail. He'd seemed secretive about it. Publish or perish, she figured.

Dakota had been impressed with his credentials, but his job wasn't what had turned her on. It was something deeper.

Ethan helped Dakota out of the car after parking under the Redondo Beach Pier. . The ocean air was crisp and cool, smelling strongly of sea salt. "We're dining at Tony's. Are you familiar with the popular restaurant located in the heart of the pier?"

Dakota nodded. "I hear great ocean views and fiery sunsets make it very romantic, but I've never eaten there."

After Ethan assisted Dakota with the tangerine sweater, she held up his navy single-breasted Pierre Cardin blazer while he slipped into it.

Ethan took Dakota's hand and began strolling leisurely toward their destination. "We don't have to be in a hurry." He looked at his watch. "We have thirty minutes before our reservations. Sunset is about an hour or so away and we definitely don't want to miss out on the spectacular view."

"The boardwalk is such a fun place, with lots of interesting things to do and see and enjoy. I ride my bike around the pier every now and then."

One thing Ethan wanted to make sure he accomplished was to purchase a candy apple for Dakota. She had told him how much she loved them and how hard they were to find around L.A. L.A. heat caused the candy to melt easily. Because he wanted her to have a nice surprise, he planned to slip away to the candy-apple stand once they were seated.

Ethan let go of Dakota's hand and put his arm around her. "Are you cold?"

"It was a bit chilly before I put on my sweater. I'm fine now."

"If you need my jacket, tell me. Don't want you freezing."

"I started to bring a lightweight jacket, but I didn't want to get bogged down with a lot of stuff. I've lived in Southern California all my life. I knew what kind of weather to expect. I promise to ask if I need your blazer."

"I'll gladly give it up. I also keep a windbreaker in the trunk, so we're prepared for how chilly it might get."

"It seems you're always prepared for everything." She liked that about him.

Ethan was an orderly person, much like she was. He was also big on anticipation, including contemplating her needs. She'd often thought he could read her mind. They also had scheduling in common. She kept a daily planner and so did he. The hours of her days were accounted for practically down to the minute. Dakota didn't like last-minute anything. Things in her life worked better when there was order.

When Ethan had phoned Dakota on the spur of the moment, the evening of the first meeting, she recalled welcoming the call. He had made his intent crystal clear before they'd finished talking. She had been interested in him from the start, loving how charismatic he was. He would've never known how much she liked him if he hadn't taken the initiative.

Ethan gave his name to the hostess stationed at the restaurant podium. The couple was immediately seated at the window table he'd requested beforehand.

After making sure Dakota was comfortably seated, he took the seat right across from her. He liked gazing into her sparkling hazel eyes, mesmerized by everything about her. His attempts to play it cool often ended in disaster. When she looked at him, his eyes betrayed him, melting into hers. The girl gave him goose bumps and caused him to have a raging fever, all at the same time. Reaching across the table, he covered her hand. "What about a glass of wine?"

Dakota smiled softly. "White merlot, please."

Ethan summoned the waiter. Once the young man appeared, he ordered the drinks. He liked wine but he preferred a chilled pomegranate martini every now and then. One was his limit when he was the designated driver.

Before Ethan got to his feet, he leaned in closer to Dakota. "Excuse me for a few minutes," he whispered in her ear.

The soft music playing overhead soothed Dakota. She couldn't believe she already missed Ethan. He hadn't been gone more than a couple of minutes. Although he hadn't said where he was off to, she assumed his absence had been necessary.

While sipping on the white merlot, she began to feel a little self-conscious. A couple of guys a table away were giving her the once-over, making her feel slightly uncomfortable. People staring at her unnerved her. She knew it was probably silly, but that's the way it was.

Ethan quickly reseated himself across from Dakota, giving her that megawatt smile she loved. Before she could blink her lashes again, he leaned across the table and kissed her gently on the cheek. "Did you miss me?"

"I did. Glad you're back." She looked over at the table with the two guys, fighting back the urge to stick her fingers in her ears and turn them back and forth. "I was a bit uncomfortable while you were gone."

Ethan looked puzzled. "Why's that?"

"The guys at the next table had fun staring me down. It made me nervous."

"You're very pretty, Dakota. Any red-blooded male would enjoy staring at you. I'd think you'd be used to it by now."

Dakota shrugged. "I'm not. Having someone eyeballing me so intently isn't something I'd want to get used to. I guess you think I'm silly."

Ethan shook his head. "Not in the least. Sorry if I gave you that impression." He briefly covered her hand with his again. "Ready to order?"

The lobster was pretty expensive but that's what Dakota wanted. She didn't have the money to offer to pay all or even half of it. "Is it okay if I order the lobster?" She felt classless as soon as the request was made.

If Dakota hadn't been serious about her query, Ethan probably would've laughed. From the look on her face, he knew he shouldn't make fun. "Order anything you want. I don't go to restaurants I can't afford."

Eyeing Ethan with open curiosity, Dakota considered his comments. "If I ever ask a guy out to dinner, I'd like to know what I'm getting my wallet into beforehand."

Disliking Dakota's comments about asking out another man, Ethan frowned. "I hope I'll be the only guy you ask out. I'd be jealous if you dated someone else."

"What exactly *are* you saying, Ethan?"

"It's simple. I don't want you to date anyone but me. Understand?"

Nervous now, she swallowed hard. "You've made yourself plain enough. What about you? Dating anyone besides me?"

Watching Dakota closely, Ethan took a sip of his martini. "I haven't asked anyone out since the first night I called you. I'm a one-woman man. I haven't dated exclusively in a long time, but I'd like to have that with you. Is it possible?"

Dakota admittedly had some issues of

trust, but she worked on that particular insecurity on a regular basis. Her heart had been broken before, a couple of times — and not just by men she'd been romantically involved with. Neither was it only men that she didn't always trust.

Dakota was flattered by Ethan's question. He seemed very sincere. She didn't want to miss out on an opportunity to be happy. The last steady boyfriend she had was over six months ago. She wasn't sure she was ready for anything exclusive, but she did love being with Ethan. If they didn't have a chance to act on their obvious chemistry, she'd never know how far things could go.

The waiter arrived at that very moment. Feeling like she'd better take the bull by the horns, Dakota decided it was best to go ahead and answer Ethan's question. He would only revisit the matter later. "About your question, I'd love to give us a chance to see if we can build toward exclusive. I like being with you. I feel special when we're together."

Ethan moved his chair closer to hers. Lifting her hand, he pressed his lips into her palm. "All we need is a chance, Dakota. I'm happy you've decided to give us one." He kissed her gently on the mouth. "I won't make you regret it."

Dakota's concentrated gaze connected with his. "I believe you."

Once Dakota finished ordering the surf and turf, lobster and steak, Ethan asked for a pound and a half of Alaskan king crab. Both ordered garden salads and baked potatoes as side dishes.

"How was your day?" Ethan asked, after the waiter disappeared.

"It has been a good one. Classes were intense and I stayed busy at work, but that makes the time go by faster. The phone lines ring nonstop, but such is life at any telemarketing job." Literally, she thought. "I have a lot of studying to do over the weekend, but I'll manage." Dakota was glad she didn't have the type of job where work piled up and had to be taken home.

What would Ethan think of her job? Just imagining it caused Dakota to shudder.

"I'm always busy at my job. It's very seldom that I don't have a backlog of work. I always feel like I'm behind even when I'm not. I'm not complaining, though. I love what I do for a living. I was born to teach."

Dakota wished she could at least halfway like what she did to earn a living.

The waiter returned to the table just as Ethan finished his comment. He carefully set down the meal in front of the appropriate diner, warning the patrons that the platters were hot. "Miss, would you like me to deshell the lobster?"

Dakota smiled up at him. "That'd be nice. Thank you."

Ethan put up his hand in a halting gesture. "I can take care of it, Dakota, if you don't mind." He glanced apologetically at the waiter.

Dakota smiled brightly. "Please, go right ahead." She smiled sweetly at the waiter.

The waiter smiled back at her knowingly as he walked away.

Ethan scowled slightly. "Sorry if I embarrassed you. I just think taking care of you is my responsibility."

"I wasn't embarrassed. And I just happen to like chivalry."

"Good. I don't want you thinking I'm possessive, 'cause I'm not."

"Stop it," she scolded gently. "Your gesture was so sweet."

"Thanks." He'd almost apologized again but stopped short. The last thing he wanted was overkill.

Ethan saw Dakota safely into the car before he went into the trunk to retrieve the surprise he'd purchased for her. He had to laugh at himself. He'd never felt this giddy over anyone.

Ethan slid into the driver's seat, holding the candy apple down, with a piece of red ribbon curled around the stick, at his left side, which made it difficult to close his car door. Turning to face her, he brought the candy apple out and handed it to her. "I got this for you. I hope you enjoy it." The smile she cast him made his insides tremble.

Leaning over the console, she kissed his cheek. "So this is why you disappeared earlier. You are too sweet. I can't believe you remembered I told you it was a favorite."

"Oh, I only go over in my head everything you say at least a couple dozen times a night." He reached over and slid the back of his hand down the side of her face "Maybe I shouldn't be telling you all that."

She laughed. "Please keep it up. I'm enjoying the flattery. I feel like I'm in a dream world when I'm with you."

"It's not a dream, Dakota, but I know what you mean. It's for real. I've never felt anything so real."

Dakota went into Ethan's arms without any prompting from him. She pulled slightly back and looked into his eyes. "It feels real to me, too. And I'm feeling you."

Dakota hadn't revealed to any man her

deep, complex layers. Ethan just might be the one male she could open up her heart to. If he kept being so attentive to her, treating her like something fragile and beautiful, she felt like she could really let herself go with him.

CHAPTER 2

Dakota looked up at the dreary gray concrete complex, wishing she didn't have to come here by herself. If her parents had survived a fatal car crash several years ago, she wouldn't be here alone. The couple had been coming home from the theater late one evening when a semi jackknifed into their car, killing them instantly. Shortly after their deaths, her parents' employer-paid medical coverage had been terminated.

Dakota had been left in charge of her eight-year-old sister, Danielle, who had Down syndrome, after their guardian/grandparents had both passed away three years ago, her grandfather dying first. Everything had fallen solely on Dakota's shoulders, just as the young woman had turned twenty-one. She was sixteen years older than Danielle.

Danni now resided at the Center of the Courageous Heart, a renowned specialized facility in Carson that treated a variety of complications arising from Down. Medicare and Medicaid paid for a good portion of Danielle's care. Because Dakota had insisted on a private facility for the child, she was responsible for all medical services the government agencies didn't cover.

Dakota stopped outside Danielle's door and said a silent prayer, asking God to keep her anxiety-free. She visited her sister practically every day, but she was overly tired this Friday evening. Working and going to school took a toll on her, but she didn't want her adorable sibling to feel any negative vibes from her. The place was as cheerful as the staff could possibly make it, but there were times when an air of gloom presided.

Just in case Danielle was napping, Dakota quietly stepped into the private room, looking straight ahead at the double bed. Her heart instantly leaped for joy. Danielle was awake and her face was lit up with the same brighter-than-gold smile she always wore for her kin. These were the kinds of moments that took away Dakota's breath.

"Kota," Danielle cried, opening her arms wide.

Scooping up Danielle into her arms, Dakota gave her a huge hug, receiving in return loving embraces and jubilant kisses. This sweet, warm child was superaffectionate. If Danni hugged or kissed someone, they knew she had handed out a little chunk of her loving heart. Dakota didn't believe her sister would ever run out of the pieces of her authentic self she exuberantly shared with others.

Dakota smiled at Danielle, lodging into her sweet little arms the brown teddy bear gift she'd brought along. Danni had quite a collection of stuffed toys and she loved each one. However, she did have a favorite: Daisy Dolly, a freckle-faced, red-haired rag doll had been Danielle's companion for years.

"Thank you, Kota." Kissing and hugging the bear, Danielle held it close.

Although Danielle had Down syndrome at birth, some of the more serious physical complications hadn't appeared until she was nearly four years old. Then all of a sudden, Danielle got sick more frequently, her health compromised to the point where she eventually required constant skilled nursing care. Home health-care nurses cared for Danni at home as long as it had been possible. Then the younger girl started to need the kind of professional assistance the older sibling was hardly equipped to provide.

Danielle called out Dakota's name again,

pointing at the cabinet where the DVDs were kept. *"Happy Feet,"* she exclaimed, giggling softly.

Dakota retrieved the movie, smiling as Danielle took the disk from her hand and inserted it into the DVD player. Dedicated professionals worked hard to help her be as independent as possible. She attended school within the facility, also participating in field trips and other special events when her health permitted.

"Can I have an orange soda, too?" Danielle spoke well. Although she sometimes had difficulty with pronunciation of complex words, she was able to communicate effectively. It was rare for her to not get her point across. Danielle was learning American Sign Language and Dakota had taken the class, too. It felt good to spend that kind of time with her sister.

Danielle hit the play button. As Dakota lay down beside her sister, sharing the same pillow, she held her hand. The siblings had seen the movie umpteen times, but neither one had tired of it. It made them laugh hysterically.

Once *Happy Feet* concluded, Danielle expressed a desire to play cards, the game of War. Dakota retrieved a deck of cards from the nightstand drawer. She then positioned the portable table across the bed. The two sisters played numerous board games, but Dakota never just allowed Danielle to win. She had to earn the winning spot in every matchup.

Dakota smoothed back Danielle's thick brown hair. It was soft and wavy in texture, much like hers. "Do you want a snack before we start?"

Danielle looked thoughtful. "Tuna sandwich and chips, please, Kota?"

Rewarding Danielle for her polite request, Dakota tenderly kissed her forehead. Using the red-tipped call button, she summoned the nursing station. When the desk clerk came over the loudspeaker, the food order was placed. "A tuna sandwich with lots of mayo, potato chips and an orange soda, please." Although all the regular staff members knew Danielle's likes and dislikes, Dakota always made sure she clearly expressed her sister's desires in case a new employee or a temp responded.

While Dakota and Danielle waited for the meal, they began the fun card game. Dakota let Danielle shuffle the cards.

"My card is bigger." Danielle clapped, laughing.

Two more cards were slapped down on the table.

"I win again," Danielle said happily.

Dakota wrinkled her nose. "My card is going to beat yours this time," she said, placing the card face up on the table. "See! I told you."

Danielle looked as happy to see Dakota win as when she won.

Her favorite card was the queen of spades. Dakota had no clue why Danielle liked that particular card so much. The competitive little girl would always sigh hard when the black queen was trumped by her sister with a king or ace. Whenever Dakota was dealt the queen of spades, Danielle didn't seem to mind. She loved her big sister and looked at her as a best friend.

Departing was hard for both sisters a couple of hours later. Whenever possible, Dakota waited until Danielle drifted off to sleep before she'd leave. The visits were normally done in two-to-three hour increments, but at times they lasted longer. Dakota also tried her best to take Danielle outside the facility for a full day at least one weekend day a month when she was physically up to the challenge.

Attending church regularly at the facility chapel also occurred. Once the religious services were over, they'd go to a local park, with a beautiful lake, and paddleboats. The girls had a blast rowing across the lake. When Danielle grew tired, Dakota had to do the work alone, but she didn't mind one iota. A variety of sandwiches, fruits, cookies, chips and drinks were brought along on the outings, neatly packed away in a small cooler. But boating and a picnic didn't hold a candle to Danielle's love of dance and music.

Mona Cassidy, a professional dance instructor, didn't charge Dakota one red cent for lessons for Danni. What she earned off students at her private dance studio made pro bono cases affordable. It was a gracious gift. Mona, in fact, taught dance to several of the kids residing at the center. She had also offered Dakota lessons so she could tap-dance with Danielle. The sisters had fun making up easy dance routines to do together.

Danielle also loved to sing and play guitar. No formal lessons for her yet, but she had been given a secondhand instrument she loved to sit and strum away on, a present from one of the nurses. Music seemed to be in the girl's blood. It was amazing to watch how she easily got into rhythm with any kind of music. She could change gears in a minute, her tiny body moving to whatever beat she heard.

Dakota entered her apartment and immediately dropped down on the sofa and stretched out. She looked up at the ceiling, thinking about her pleasant visit with Danielle. Rarely were the visits unpleasant. The little girl had so much love inside her and loved giving it away. Dakota recalled her parents saying they had to give love away to keep it.

Even though she always tried hard not to think about it, Dakota wondered what it might've been like for the family had Sonya and Thomas survived. The warm and loving couple had doted on each other and their two girls. Thomas had been a good father and his girls had meant everything to him. He had referred to them as his precious blossoms from God.

Explaining to Danielle what tragedy had befallen their parents was the most difficult and worst task Dakota had ever taken on. She shook her head from side to side, trying to stave off the horrific memories.

The phone rang, causing Dakota to groan softly. During her times of bittersweet reflection she didn't like to talk on the phone. The frequent calls she received from the health facility didn't give her the luxury of ignoring the phone. She checked the caller ID. Ethan.

"Did I call at a bad time?" Ethan asked.

"You didn't. I'm stretched out on the sofa and reflecting on some things. What're you up to?"

"I was into some deep thinking, too, thoughts about you. Do you roller-skate?"

She laughed. "Yeah, but I haven't skated in a long while. I was pretty good at it. Are we talking about roller-skating or in-line?"

Ethan chuckled. "Plain old roller-skating."

Dakota had fun conjuring up an image of sophisticated Ethan on skates. "It's really been a long time. Hopefully it'd be just like riding a bike, something we don't forget how to do."

"How about joining my friends and me this evening at On Four Wheels, a roller rink located in my neighborhood? I'd like to introduce you to the folks I hang out with."

"Are you willing to risk total embarrassment? Like I said, I haven't skated in years. You could spend the entire evening picking me up off the floor."

Ethan grinned broadly. "I'd love to play your hero." He'd have to get used to his sudden desire to be gallant. A hero, he wasn't. "Whether you're on your feet or falling on your sweet bottom, I won't be embarrassed. I can pick you up around six-thirty."

Dakota laughed. "I haven't agreed yet, but if I do, I'll just meet you there. And thanks for saying I won't embarrass you. But if I fall on my butt, I'll feel enough shame for us both." She glanced at her watch, knowing she really did want to be with him.

Ethan decided not to question her comment about meeting him at the rink, but it had aroused his curiosity. "Come on, now. Be a good sport. If you prefer not to skate, you don't have to. But I'd still like you to be a part of my evening."

"You've just made the offer more tempting. I'll seriously consider the skating part, but you can count me in as a spectator for now. Thanks for thinking of me. Care to tell me a bit about your friends and what I should expect?"

"A little worried about my buddies perhaps?" Ethan queried.

"Just want to know if I should worry or not."

"I understand perfectly. My friends are great. You can expect genuine, down-to-earth folks who all care about each other. In some capacity, we're all employed by the California education systems. Everyone is single and close to becoming thirty. We all hang out regularly. I can assure you everyone is friendly."

"Sounds like a great start to the evening. I'll see you at the rink, Ethan."

"I can hardly wait. See you there."

As Dakota hung up the receiver, she thought about meeting Ethan's friends. Even though they'd dated only a short time, he hadn't gone into any great detail about his buddies. She was curious about them. He'd said they were great, so she wondered why he hadn't told her more about them before now.

Perhaps he hadn't said much for the same reason I hadn't mentioned Danielle.

It was just too soon for Ethan to meet her sister. From what she knew about the dating game, couples meeting family members didn't come prematurely. When it did happen, it was normally after a couple's relationship had turned serious.

The thought of what to wear entered Dakota's mind. Jeans were more appropriate, just in case, she considered. Even if she had been a pretty good skater in her youth, she shouldn't count on that. In fact, she couldn't recall the last time she'd been roller-skating.

Dakota remembered her first boyfriend and skating partner, Anthony Qualls, as she rifled through her closet. He had hurt her feelings during her junior year in high school, when he'd been stolen away by the pretty and vivacious Jasmine Walters.

Well, no one could've stolen him away had he really been mine.

Anthony had gotten a big payback. Less than two months later Jasmine had ended up leaving him for the buff football captain.

Justice had prevailed.

Dakota gave a fleeting thought to all the people she'd lost in one way or another, which were attributed to many of her fears. Boyfriends and girlfriends would come and go, but the loss of parents and grandparents was incomparable.

After removing a pair of freshly laundered boot-cut blue jeans from a hanger in her cramped closet, Dakota found the navy-and-burgundy striped V-neck sweater. Navy leather flats were chosen over sneakers. After choosing a coordinating dark blue sweater, in case the rink was cold, she laid everything out on the bed and went into the bathroom to shower.

Ethan rolling around on his own shiny black skates held fast Dakota's attention.

She thought he was an excellent roller skater and he looked so good. Strictly coincidental, he also wore dark blue jeans and a Sean John navy-and-burgundy striped shirt, open at the collar. He appeared relaxed and confident. Because she hadn't decided on skating yet, she eyed other patrons to see how well they maneuvered. A polished wooden railing skirting the entire perimeter kept spectators separated from the skating surface.

The idea to bring Danielle there one day to watch the skaters quickly skipped across her mind. Maybe she could learn to skate, too. If nothing else, she knew her sister would be excited by the mere possibility. Dakota could already envision the flaming show of fireworks in her baby sister's eyes if she simply mentioned it.

Dakota waved at Ethan and smiled as he rolled by.

Ethan quickly exited the floor and came over to where Dakota stood at the spectators' railing. Taking her into his arms, he gave her a warm hug and a passionate kiss. "How long have you been here? I've been watching out for you."

"Long enough to check out your skating skills. You're good."

"Thank you." Ethan looked around when he heard his name. "Those are my friends. Everyone is dying to meet you." He took her by the hand. "Don't be nervous."

Ethan's group came right over to meet the

woman their friend was so taken with.

Ethan bumped one of the guys with his shoulder. "This is Maxwell Harper, my best friend since kindergarten, the comedian in the bunch. He's also a great world history teacher at a high school magnate program."

Smiling, Dakota extended her hand to Maxwell. "It's a pleasure meeting you."

Ethan pointed at one of the women. "Charlene Rhodes, Max's girlfriend, is a special-education teacher. Dakota is working toward a career in the same field. You two already have something in common," he said to Charlene.

"That's great to hear," Charlene said. "There is such a shortage of good teachers in special ed. If you ever have any questions about the field, please feel free to ask me."

"Thanks, Charlene. I'll probably have a lot to ask about. It's a fascinating career."

Ethan presented to Dakota the rest of his friends. "Rudy Cantos is my old college roommate. He and our lovely Maria Castro are engaged to be married and Mandy Harris and Todd Williams have been dating a couple of months. Mandy is a long-standing member of our group, the only female. Maxwell, Rudy and I are also fraternity brothers."

Dakota's smile was genuinely friendly. She

was nervous, but she didn't come across as such. "It's nice to meet all of you. I'm looking forward to our evening."

The ladies immediately put Dakota at ease. The guys went off together to let the women get a little better acquainted.

"Are you going to skate?" Maria asked Dakota.

Ethan and his friends appeared to be having so much fun that Dakota easily made up her mind, giving Maria a positive response.

She excused herself and quickly made her way to the rental area. "Size six-and-a-half," she told the teenaged girl behind the counter. "I prefer the white skates over the brown ones."

"Sure thing. Are you planning on wearing socks?"

"I am." Dakota looked puzzled. "Is that a problem?"

"It might be if you don't go up at least a half size. The seven will work better with socks. Otherwise, the fit might be kind of snug."

With her rental skates in hand, Dakota found an empty bench and sat down to lace up. Her parents had also loved to skate. They'd accompany Dakota to the rink when she was younger. She smiled wistfully.

Maria, Charlene and Mandy came over to where Dakota was.

"How's it coming?" Mandy asked. "We came back to see if you're ready to hit the floor."

"Ouch," Dakota said, grimacing playfully. "That's the last thing I want to do. I haven't done this in a while."

"You'll do okay," Maria encouraged. "You can't be any worse than me. I fall all the time."

"We all do. Just have fun with it," Charlene suggested.

"Thanks for the pep talk." Dakota got to her feet but was a bit shaky.

Maria and Charlene got on either side of Dakota.

"We're here to help you. It'll be all right," Mandy remarked.

Grateful for the kindness shown to her, Dakota smiled. "Okay. Here goes."

Mandy reached down and picked up Dakota's shoes. "I'll put these in the locker with the rest of ours. We never pay for two."

After slipping twice, Dakota wasn't so positive she'd made the right decision. Slowly and carefully she made her way around the huge rink, staying close to the railing. Teetering to the left and tottering to the right had her fearful. Her butt kissing the floor would mortify her. Moving even closer in to the railing, she slid her arm alongside it to help keep her upright. She thought about retraining herself upstairs where the children's floor was located. It would be safer.

An arm slid unexpectedly about Dakota's waist, startling her, causing her to nearly topple over. As she looked up at Ethan, her eyes gave him a slight warning shot. "You scared me . . . and I almost fell. I can't afford to break any bones."

Ethan looked sheepish. "Sorry about that. But I recall someone telling me they could skate. Or did I just imagine it?" His eyes gleamed with boyish mischief.

"What I said is that *it was probably like riding a bike, something you never forget.* I also mentioned your getting embarrassed if you had to pick me up."

Ethan's eyes suddenly locked into Dakota's hot, melting gaze. In his ears the silence was loud as a lion's roar. As he had blocked out the overhead music, all he wanted to hear was the sound of her sweet voice. Her eyes, startled with surprise, had captured him in their brightness. Her pretty face was creamy and soft as silk.

The enchanting expression on Ethan's

handsome face caused Dakota to tremble within. The intimate feel of his concerted gaze caused a rosy blush to spread over her cheeks. No one had ever looked at her the way he did. It made her feel good.

Ethan's fingers itched to flit tenderly across Dakota's lips. His mouth desired to kiss hers until each gasped for air. He couldn't count the times he'd imagined himself kissing her passionately, his tongue coiling around hers. Holding her tenderly in his arms, they'd dance to music only they could hear. He knew he needed to snap out of this trancelike state he found himself in, but he didn't want this special moment to end. Staring into this sexy woman's eyes actually brought amazing peace to his spirit.

Tearing her eyes away from the intensity of Ethan's came hard for Dakota, but she was the first one to break what had seemed like a magic spell. The tender way he looked at her had increased her trembling. She imagined that gently smoothing his face with the back of her hand would bring her sweet solace, but she wasn't that bold. Their physical desires were quickly becoming an ever-brewing passion, waiting impatiently to break loose, giving them freedom to touch, kiss and explore each other's body the electrifying way lovers did.

Would they eventually become lovers? Dakota couldn't help but wonder.

This felt like old times for Dakota, fun times, when her life was carefree and full of laughter. All the family responsibilities had belonged to her parents back then. Accomplishing her homework and light chores around the house was it for her. She had a mother and father and she hadn't had to act as a single mother to a small girl while going to school and working.

The feelings of clumsiness and fear of falling had just upped and left Dakota. Her legs were steady now. Tickled pink that her skills hadn't been forgotten, she smiled broadly. Perhaps Ethan skating beside her, his arm lodged snugly against her waist, had unleashed her confidence. Reclaiming her ability to skate was like riding a bike. She hadn't forgotten. The fluid smoothness in which she now moved allowed her to relax.

Loud, with ear-piercing bass, a fast-paced Usher song, "Yeah," suddenly blasted from the speakers, knocking Dakota off stride. As Ethan's feet picked up speed, he practically dragged her around the floor. As a sharp turn loomed in front of her, she fought hard to stay on her feet. His speed was too much for her to keep up with. Then her feet got tangled up with his and both went down hard.

The heat stealing into Dakota's face felt like a raging inferno had come to claim her. She could only guess what Ethan must think of her clumsiness. If only she'd been able to keep up with him. He had already gotten to his feet, but she was still too mortified to move a muscle.

Ethan stretched his hand down to her. "Are you okay? Are you hurt? This is my fault. Please let me help you up."

Dakota shook her head, but she couldn't look up at him or take his hand. Getting to her feet under her own power was a bit more valiant for her. It might also help her save face. At the very least, she felt compelled to give it the old college try.

Dakota failed to make it to her feet on the first and second attempts. Looking totally out of sync, she finally took hold of Ethan's hand. Feeling silly, she thanked him, wishing her voice had been stronger. No sooner than she'd thought she could stand on her own two feet, her legs flew out from under her again. In grabbing for her date's hand, she took him down again. Dakota didn't know whether to laugh or cry. Bawling like a baby definitely wasn't appropriate, especially when it was funny.

Ethan suddenly busted up into deep, guttural laughter. His rolling hilarity was so infectious that Dakota couldn't help but join in. Before she even tried to get up again, his friends had surrounded them, sounding like a pack of wolves howling at the moon.

With his laughter under control now, Ethan got to his feet. Sympathy for her was awash in his eyes. Then he and Maxwell took a hold of each one of Dakota's hands and helped her up. After accompanying her off the floor, they went over to a wooden bench, where she sat down to try to regroup. The three women were also sensitive to her plight, which did a lot to lessen Dakota's embarrassment. Dakota no longer felt that she'd shamed Ethan.

Just have fun with it. You'll do okay with it. I fall all the time. We all do.

As Dakota recalled the kind remarks the ladies had said to her earlier, she knew she was overreacting to the mishap. This was all in fun. There was nothing to be embarrassed about. Deciding not to give it another ounce of thought, she cautiously got to her feet. Before Ethan had a chance to take hold of her hand, she was making her way back to the arena floor. Favoring triumph over failure, Dakota was determined to not allow the latter to stake its claim. The huge surge of confidence made her feel powerful and in total control.

Grinning broadly, shaking his head, Ethan watched after Dakota. His eyes shone with pride and his heart began to fill with it. She wasn't a quitter. It was one of her many qualities he liked. Determination was something else they had in common.

Once Dakota skated uneventfully around the rink a couple of times, Ethan rejoined her, careful not to startle her. He gently grasped her hand, brought it up to his lips and kissed the back of it. "You did great, kid. I'm so proud of you."

"Thanks." Dakota blushed, smiling at the same time.

A spicy voice suddenly came over the loudspeaker to announce a couples-only skate. The overhead lights had dimmed simultaneously. Alicia Keys's powerful voice sweeping over the arena was exciting. "A Woman's Worth" was the moving selection.

Ethan put his arm around Dakota's waist and pulled her closer to him. "Think we can do this?"

Dakota smiled flirtatiously. "I know we can."

As the couple began moving over the floor

in perfect harmony, his hand tightened on her waist. Her heart rate quickened once again. His touch was tender and reassuring. The uniting of eyes ignited fiery sparks, but the union lasted only a moment. The flow of heavy traffic made them concentrate. Neither wanted another collision.

The small group of friends was seated in the concession stand area, each sipping on cold drinks. No one had ordered food since Maxwell had brought up the idea of stopping by their favorite pizza haunt before calling it a night. The rink was due to close in thirty minutes. Everyone had agreed to hang around until then.

Ethan was especially fond of the idea to stay until closing because it meant he could whirl around the floor with Dakota a little longer. He loved holding her hand and keeping her close to him.

As Ethan looked over at Dakota, his eyes were instantly drawn to her plump mouth. The kisses they'd shared thus far had been sweet and innocent and only one had been slightly probing. The way her full, luscious lips caressed the straw she sipped from had his imagination running wild.

Maybe it would happen tonight, Ethan thought. Then he recalled she'd driven herself there and he wouldn't be taking her home. Just the thought of it was like a dousing of ice water onto a naked body stranded outdoors in the dead of winter.

Anthony's Pizzeria was jam-packed and lively when Ethan and his friends arrived. Because another large group of folks was just leaving, they quickly grabbed the table, feeling lucky to land the vacated seats.

Booming music and a bunch of fun-loving patrons had the place lit up. Loud talking and gales of laughter came from every area of the place. A karaoke session was just about to begin, a regular part of the entertainment lineup. Performers were lousy for the most part, but there were some singers who possessed record label potential.

Dakota was now very comfortable with Ethan's girlfriends. She felt included in their little group and it didn't feel at all like a clique. The ladies decided to get into the bathroom before the karaoke session began.

Dakota washed her hands and dried them on a paper towel. "Have any of you ever done karaoke?" Dakota asked, removing lip gloss from her purse.

Charlene threw her head back and laughed. "We've got up there and made fools of ourselves countless times. We don't care that none of us can sing. We just like to have fun. What about you? Have you ever got onstage?"

"No, but I think that's about to change. What do you think Ethan will say if I get up there and sing?"

"He'll love it," Mandy assured her. "Ethan and the other guys are game for a lot of crazy stuff. Don't be surprised by anything we do."

"We work hard all week and play even harder on the weekends," Charlene said.

"Now, what I want to know is, can you sing?" Maria queried.

Grinning, Dakota shrugged and winked. "I think I'll let you all be the judge of that. Either way, I'm not ready for the good time to end. I keep hearing everyone saying it's all about fun. I've bought into it now. I'm sold."

"Let's do this," Mandy enthused. "I can't wait to see if you can sing or not."

As the ladies howled and hooted, high fives were passed all around.

Ethan noticed how antsy Dakota had become all of a sudden. It made him wonder if she had a yen to sing. But the sign of reluctance glowing in her eyes was also easy enough for him to read. If she was content to sit there and cheer on the others, whether their performances were good or bad, he wasn't going to push her to get up onstage.

A couple of minutes after the orders had been taken, Dakota nudged Ethan to get his attention.

He turned to look at her. "Are you okay? You seem a little antsy."

She pointed at the stage. "Will I embarrass you if I get up there and sing?"

His eyes brightened. "Stop worrying about embarrassing me. I want you to enjoy yourself." He leaned in and kissed her cheek. "Go for it!" He didn't ask her if she could sing. It didn't matter to him. All he wanted was for them to have a great time.

Quite a few of the males went crazy when Dakota stepped up onstage.

Ethan thought the wolf whistlers had great taste, but they'd have to take a backseat tonight. Dakota Faraday was there with him.

Once Dakota made her song choice, she picked up the microphone. Blowing kisses to the crowd and bowing, she acted out the part of a diva. Losing all of her inhibitions, she tossed her hair around and let the music enter her soul. None of this would've been easy without the encouragement from Ethan and his friends. Dakota didn't know she could have such a good time — and she didn't want this night to end.

Everyone talked about fun and Dakota wanted to show them she'd gotten it.

Ethan didn't realize he was holding his breath until he was forced to release it. He was nervous for her. Audiences could be cruel and he didn't know how she'd react if they heckled her. As she hit the first few notes of the song, he felt himself go lax. The girl had it. She hadn't gone onstage just to be up there. Dakota had something to offer.

As she seductively belted out Beyoncé's version of the old classic "Fever," that's exactly what Ethan and every other male in the place felt. Dakota put on a show she didn't know she was capable of. She knew she could sing, but never in her wildest dreams did she think she'd get up in front of a crowd like this. She had a ball with her magical performance. Dakota's goal was to make sure everyone else did, too.

Then, Dakota suddenly turned her smoldering and seductive eyes on Ethan. The message he received let him know she had come down with a fever, too. Only he could bring down her temperature.

■ ■ ■ ■

Ethan stood up and kissed Dakota to welcome her back to the table. The ladies were beside themselves with joy as they jumped up to give her warm hugs. Dakota was glad she'd been able to show everyone she was game, too.

All the guys quickly left the table and rushed the stage. They had gotten pumped up during Dakota's performance and now it was time for them to show off. Ethan grabbed the microphone and mussed his hair, making an Elvis-like stance. Rudy strummed a nonexistent guitar and Maxwell and Todd had everyone cheering on their fancy, animated footwork.

"All Shook Up" was the song they'd chosen.

Dakota couldn't believe her ears as she recalled thinking of how Ethan had her feeling: all shook up. Tears of joy filled her eyes. No longer would she dwell on what she'd missed out on. All she'd think about now was what was next on her social agenda.

Dakota now had firsthand knowledge that Ethan and his boys were regular cutups. Maxwell was hardly the only comedian and Ethan was an absolute riot. She hadn't seen this funny, engaging side of him before now. She knew he had a great sense of humor, but his sharp wit and quick verbal comebacks had been downright hilarious and intriguing. Ethan and his crew had been successful at making her laugh until it hurt.

At fifteen minutes before midnight, Ethan leaned against the outside door of Dakota's apartment. He had followed her home to make sure she got there safely.

Wrapping her up in his arms, he looked deep into her eyes, kissing her gently. The next kiss deepened, escalating his heart rate. The third kiss was all he'd hoped for. With a beautiful, sexy woman like Dakota he could easily lose his self-control. So far she had only agreed to build toward an exclusive relationship and he had to respect that. In his heart he already believed she was a woman worth waiting for.

Dakota smiled brilliantly. "I had a beautiful time with you and your friends. I think I passed their muster."

"I know you did. You were a big hit, lady. Think I can get an encore of the song you sang at the pizza place?"

"You were a big hit, too, with me. As for the encore, I hope we'll have many." Laughing inwardly at how his mouth had fallen agape, she wiggled out of his arms and unlocked the front door. "Goodnight, Ethan. Hope we'll talk soon."

"Lady, you can bet money on it."

CHAPTER 3

Ethan always felt much better after a hot shower, yet the back of his neck still had a crook in it. He'd love to have it massaged out. It was too late to get it taken care of tonight. He'd call in the morning and get an appointment with his therapist.

Dakota had soft hands. He easily imagined her massaging his tight muscles. Her fingers were strong. They'd held on tightly to his digits during the initial fall at the roller rink a couple of days ago, he recalled. Her hands were also as tender as their strength. The tenderness was what he remembered best. Every time she'd touched him he had felt it right down to the center of his core.

A glance at the clock let him know it was too late to phone Dakota. He didn't want to risk disrespecting her, but it was difficult to ignore the strong desire he had to hear her voice. Whenever he talked to her, he got caught up in her gentle, soothing tone.

Instead of picking up the phone, Ethan settled for getting deeper in thought about the evening he'd spent in Dakota's company at the roller rink. She had been a megahit with all his friends, especially Maxwell, who'd said he definitely would've asked her out had he met her first. The two friends had a rule to never date anyone the other one had been involved with, no matter how casual or serious the relationship was.

Once Dakota had gotten over her embarrassment of falling down, he remembered how she had shown the valiant side of her. Her show of character had made her a major leaguer with Ethan and his friends. Although he still thought she was somewhat reserved, he hoped her demeanor toward him would change as she got to know him.

To distract himself from calling Dakota, he walked down the hall to his office and pulled out a folder from the filing cabinet built into the el extension of his desk. Bent on perusing its content, which held the work he'd done so far on his book, he carried the file back to the living room. After turning on the television set, he made himself comfortable on the sofa, propping pillows behind his back before stretching out fully.

Ethan turned his attention back to the folder. After reviewing the first couple of dozen or so pages, he was unable to concentrate further. He closed the folder and set it aside, taking a quick glance at the clock.

Before Ethan could change his mind again about calling Dakota, he grabbed the receiver and dialed her number, hoping she was still awake. As her sweet voice instantly brought a generous smile to his lips, an audible sigh of relief followed.

"Glad you're still up. I've been dying to talk to you. How was your day?"

"I'm glad, too. Wouldn't want to miss your call. My day has been busy but good. I accomplished a lot of must-do things. I was just about to turn off the light. Normally I don't go to sleep until after the late-night talk show. When I don't have to get up early, I stay up until the wee hours. I love to read before settling in."

"That makes two of us. I either read or write before shutting down. I've been doing a lot of research on the computer this evening. I already mentioned my project to you." He hadn't told her the subject matter of his work. His curiosity was strong about an industry very few people knew exactly how it worked or how to go about breaking into it.

"That's great! I'm sure you're excited about getting tenure?"

"It'll be nice. I'm working my butt off to earn it."

"It's just a matter of time. You should be proud of yourself. I'm proud of you."

"Thanks. That's nice to know. When can I see you again?"

She smiled, happy he'd asked. "Maybe you should tell me when."

"If it wasn't so late, I'd say tonight. I miss you. What about tomorrow evening? We can either go out to dinner or I can cook for us at my place. I'm a decent chef."

"Dining in or out is okay with me. You decide. I'm excited about seeing you."

Dakota's last statement made Ethan feel good inside. He was excited, too, more than she knew. "Call you tomorrow with the details. Cool?"

"Noon is a good time to call my cell. There's a long break between classes. What was your day like?" Dakota asked.

"Crazy, like all my days are. I love my job, but my students are a handful. I have several outspoken ones, mainly the females. Getting them to stop talking long enough to listen to me is a daunting task. They usually have the last word."

"I find that one hard to believe, Ethan. To me, you seem like a man in control."

"I wish I was more in control in these

71

instances. Sparring with these particular sisters can wear down a brother." Ethan chuckled. "Sometimes I just want them to stop talking before I stop breathing."

"Well, in that case, I don't want you to stop breathing on me. I'd love for you to stick around."

"That was sweet of you, Dakota. I want to continue hanging out with you. But I'll let you go."

"Have a good night, Ethan. I'll look forward to your call."

"Me, too. Good night."

Ethan suddenly felt displeased with himself. There were specific questions he wanted to ask Dakota, but once again, he'd held back. Being clueless about her and who she was and why she kept him at a safe distance wouldn't set them on the right track. Snatching up the receiver, he hit the redial button, sure she hadn't gone to sleep that fast.

"It's me again. Can we talk? I mean *really* talk?"

Dakota felt apprehension creeping in. "Is something wrong? What is it?"

"I don't know. I feel so damn good when I'm with you, but everything doesn't feel right. Is there something about me you're uncomfortable with? If so, I'd like to know what it is. Something's standing between us. What can it be?"

Contemplating her response, Dakota pressed her trembling fingers into her lips. "You're right. I'm standing in between us and so are my past experiences. I'm afraid of getting my heart broken again. Can you guarantee me that that won't happen with you?"

"I wish I could. I think you know better than that. Please tell me what happened. Maybe it'll start the healing process."

Dakota blew out a stream of shaky breath. "What happened to me occurred months ago. The betrayal still feels current. A couple of gal pals betrayed me in ways I'd never stoop so low to return the favor. One of my so-called best girlfriends, Lori Taylor, had taken up with my boyfriend, Everett Washington, while we were still dating. They'd been going at each other long before I found out."

Ethan heard the raw pain in her voice. "That's the toughest kind of heartbreak."

Dakota knew worse heartaches, but she didn't want to overwhelm him. "I was having a hard time when we met. I've been through a lot of stuff. Two people I trusted most disappointed me deeply."

"You mentioned a couple of gal pals. Who

was the other one?"

"Mercy Winters claimed to be a best friend. She stole convenience checks sent to me by my credit card company and tried to cash one for a big sum, which would've gone against my card. Suspicious of the check, her bank took the appropriate action. It's a long story. I was stunned when she wasn't prosecuted. It was simply put on her credit report that she'd committed check fraud. Yet another bitter disappointment to deal with."

"Everyone who calls themselves *friend* doesn't always meet the criteria. Do you still have feelings for the guy who hurt you?"

"None whatsoever. I'm cautious. Maybe overly cautious, but it has everything to do with me and nothing to do with you. I believe you're trustworthy."

Ethan was glad she wasn't harboring feelings for the heartbreaker. That wouldn't have felt so good to learn. "So tell me what I need to do to get closer to you and to help you get through the bad stuff, past and present."

"Patience is all that I ask of you. Is that doable?"

"Absolutely. I want us to get to know each other on a deeply personal level. Then we'll feel free to talk more about our triumphs and the challenges we face. I want you to be able to talk to me about anything. Problems aren't ever resolved with silence."

Persia listened to George with total disinterest. Her day had been tiring and all she wanted to do was get home and sleep. Soon after he'd asked her name, the client started in on his wife by whining and complaining about her expecting him to be superman.

"She's certainly no superwoman. The lady is horrible in bed and she never wants to try anything new. The same position every time gets old. She's boring when it comes to creativity. She's so scared the children will hear what goes on. The master is downstairs and the three kids sleep upstairs. They can't hear a thing."

"Do you still love her?"

The caller paused, as if caught off guard by the pointed question. While thinking about his response, he scratched his head. "Don't get me wrong, I love my wife. It's just that she's such a prude. But why talk about my wife?"

"At least say something kind about her. She's the mother of your three kids. You brought up your wife to me, remember?"

"I did, didn't I? But why do you care whether I respect my wife or not? You're not respecting her by talking sexy to her husband over the phone."

Persia knew she hadn't said one sexy word to George. He had yet to give her an opportunity. Besides that, she preferred to let the callers set the stage and choose the subject matter for the conversations. "Hey, you dialed my number." She bit down on her tongue.

In the silence, she wondered if she'd said too much.

"Have you ever thought about becoming a marriage counselor, Persia? I think you'd make a good one," George remarked, sounding downright stupid and not caring.

Persia scowled. "What? Are you kidding me?"

"Guys just need to blow off a head of steam at times. My wife *is* a real good homemaker. She's crazy about the kids." He paused. "Do you think I'm wrong for calling phone-sex lines?"

George had put himself on a guilt trip, Persia thought. He already knew he was dead wrong. No one had to tell him that either. And it certainly wasn't her place to enlighten him. She was in the business to meet her obligations, not to lose clients. If she told him he was wrong and he stopped calling, she'd lose a client and a good chunk of change. Persia couldn't afford it.

"Are you still there?" George asked, sounding anxious.

With impatience rising in her again, Persia sighed inwardly. "I'm here. Do you want to keep up with this conversation or are you ready to get it on?"

George paused again for a couple of moments. "First off, I want to know what you look like. Then I want to hear in detail exactly what you're wearing."

"My skin is silky, the color of dark chocolate, yet it's sweet as honey, not a bit bitter. I'm a statuesque five foot seven, with the perkiest thirty-eight C breasts, real ones. My derriere is so firm and tight a quarter would bounce off it — and so is my flat stomach, with a diamond stud in my belly button. With golden-brown eyes and long, dark brown hair, I turn on lots of men. As for what I'm wearing, I'm in my favorite outfit, my birthday suit."

His breath coming hard, George had to suck in air. "I guess I should go now. This is my first call to you and guilt is busy kicking my butt. Before I hang up, could you whisper something sweet in my ear, something real sweet yet kinda kinky?"

"George." Her voice had turned low and throaty, sexy and hot. For fun, she'd strongly emphasized the Southern accent. "I'd love to pour chocolate syrup all over your sexy body and then spray you with whipped cream. From head to toe, I'd lick off every bit. How'd that sound?"

"I love it. Will you marry me, Persia?"

"Sure, George, whenever you divorce your wife. Call me when it's final."

George laughed. "I really like you and your sense of humor. Is it possible for us to talk again or do I hook up with a different lady every time I call?"

"You can talk to me again." Persia gave George her personal code and then called out to him her work schedule. She hoped she'd landed a regular, but George's guilt over calling a sex line might get to him.

"Hope we talk soon." Sounding totally satisfied, George hung up.

Persia had barely hung up the phone when it buzzed loudly in her ear again. Wondering why she'd been given another call so close to the end of her shift, she reluctantly answered the line. George should've been the last caller of the evening, she grumbled mentally, though she knew she needed to earn as much as possible.

"Hello," she breathed in her sultriest voice. "What's on your sweet mind?"

"You," was the simple reply, yet strong

and commanding. "I finally got up the nerve to call you. I've been thinking about you all day. Your commercial is hot and provocative. I love the shot with the chains. How would you use those chains on me?"

"Any way you'd like. Chaining you to a bed comes to mind. Then I can have my way with you, any way I like it."

"Naughty girl is what you are. What kind of toys do you have?"

"All kinds. If I don't have your preference, I'll get it just for you."

Persia hadn't ever had anyone talk to her about chains or other kinky stuff. This brassy man made her feel uncomfortable. She was used to the shier guys, the ones who preferred her to set the tempo, like George.

Despite his comment about "getting up the nerve to call in," he sounded sure of himself. Persia wasn't the sexy woman in the commercials the caller had referred to, but clients weren't privy to that information. Professional models and actresses were used to shoot advertising spots. Besides the obvious, commercials were also done for visual effects. They provided men with a face and body to fantasize about during conversations.

Although many women who worked at

Licensed to Thrill were beautiful and sexy, they simply weren't the actual ladies used in the ads. The intent wasn't for workers and clients to hook up in person, though it did happen quite often.

"By the way, my name is Luke Lockhart. I'm a huge star in adult films. I'm sure you've seen me before. That is, if you watch soft porn." He paused. "Have you ever had a lesbian encounter?" the man asked.

"I haven't seen you before, Luke, but I'm sure you're good at what you do."

"I'm an expert, the hottest ticket around in adult films," he boasted.

If that was the case, Persia had to wonder why Luke was calling a phone-sex line. "I'd think you'd get enough sex in your line of work. What made you call in?"

"Like I said, your commercial is smoking hot. I work with a lot of different women, but I'm not attracted to them. Besides, I wouldn't want a woman who does what I do for a living."

Coming from someone in the same profession, Persia thought it was interesting. "When did you get into the adult film industry?"

"I was a senior in high school. A friend's older brother turned me on to it. At eighteen, I was attracted to money. Do you have fantasies about becoming a porn star?"

Persia felt sorry for any guy who'd trashed his youth and body for easy money. She couldn't imagine anything about his profession as easy. "Afraid not."

"If you're open to what I'm into, the paychecks are off the chain."

Persia blew out a shaky breath. "I'm always open to getting paid," she said quite honestly. "I'm only here to talk." Persia was comfortable with her answer, and she couldn't be accused of lying to or misleading a client.

"Bet I can change your mind, with time," he taunted.

For the next forty-five minutes Persia talked with Luke. The conversation never got into anything hot and sexy, considering how it'd started out. It was tame and normal, reminding her of two friends talking about the day-to-day issues in their lives. He was more into asking her questions about her job, which was kind of odd. It also gave her the impression he might be a recruiter for the adult film industry. That made more sense.

Persia was glad when the phone call finally ended. His lifestyle wasn't something she was interested in, no matter how much money it paid. Putting her alter ego to bed at the end of the workday always felt good, up until she had to reawaken her.

As Ethan welcomed Dakota into his home, he gave her several sweet kisses. "You look marvelous. You wear red very well. I love the dress."

Dakota did a full turn to show off her simple but lovely red sheath. "I thank you." She looked him over from head to toe. "It looks like I'm a bit overdressed. Had I known you were wearing jeans I would've done the same."

"Oh, no, you made the perfect choice. I love feminine fluff. I can change clothes if you'd like me to."

Dakota shook her head. "I like you just the way you are."

"Good. Let me show you around before we sit down to dinner."

Dakota took the arm Ethan extended to her. He had told her he was a neat one. And he had told the absolute truth. There didn't seem to be a thing out of place.

"This is my formal living room, an area no one ever comes into. Maybe I need to buy some furniture so I can use it. You think?"

"That would help make it serviceable," Dakota joked.

"I'm definitely more comfortable in the family room, where I can watch the big screen, lounging on the leather sofa or kicking back on the recliners. Maybe I'll get you to help me pick out furniture for both formals. My dining room is empty, too."

As Dakota received the dime tour, she saw that Ethan favored darker woods but lighter colored furniture and glass tabletops. The leather furnishings were a light tan. Various shades of beige and brown were prevalent throughout. Entryways were designed in dramatic arches. The kitchen appliances were all black with stainless steel trim and the walls had been painted a mustard shade, which provided a bold contrast. The center island was where she imagined Ethan preparing his food.

His hands turned upward in an encompassing gesture. "This is where I hang out every day. I'm glad you accepted my invitation. I'll show you the bedrooms and my office after dinner. Think you can stand the suspense for that long?"

Dakota took hold of his hand. "Eager anticipation is always a good thing."

"Hmm. I really like the sound of that."

Ethan had set a lovely kitchen table, creating a romantic ambience for him and Dakota to dine by. Several candles had been lit and placed all about the room. Once he said a blessing over the food, he poured into crystal glasses a crisp white wine complementary to the seafood.

Steamed snow crab legs, grilled shrimp, rice pilaf and the fresh salad Ethan had prepared for dinner looked very appetizing.

Dakota had put a nice portion of everything on her plate. A little worried about getting butter sauce on her dress, she shielded it with a couple of napkins. Ethan cracked the crab for her. Removing the meat from the shell with a fork, he placed it on her plate.

Dakota liked the attentiveness, loved how well Ethan treated her. He seemed to enjoy doing nice things for her and he also liked to make her smile. Being in his company was a tremendous joy for her, just as her presence was for him. When he'd asked for them to talk more, she hadn't thought it was an unreasonable request. Dakota hoped she could open up to him about everything, but she knew it wouldn't come all at once.

A few minutes later Dakota put seconds of everything but crab on her plate. "This rice pilaf is the best I've ever eaten. You have to teach me how to make it."

"I'd love to. It's simple. I'm pleased you

like the food."

"Everything is delicious. Mind pouring me a little more wine?"

"At your service, my lady."

"Are you originally from California, Ethan?"

"Born and raised not too far from here. I graduated from Torrance High School and went to the University of California, Dominguez Hills."

"I hope to transfer there in the winter term. It's close enough to my apartment for me to walk to classes."

"You could, but I don't recommend it. Things aren't the way they used to be. There are folks out there just looking for trouble. Daylight isn't a deterrent anymore."

"I know how rough things are these days."

"That's good to know." Ethan looked closely at her. "We've been dating, but we don't know a whole lot about each other. What's your favorite color? I don't even know your birthday yet."

"Anything I look good in and whatever color I have on at the time is my favorite. I'm a January baby, just barely. January thirty-first. I'm an Aquarius, the water bearer."

"Figure that. I'm a February boy. Our birth dates are only one day apart, but not quite six years. I'm the same sign as you. Are Aquarians compatible?"

Dakota smiled at his inquisitive expression. "Don't know. I've never dated one. I'll guess we'll soon find out."

Ethan grinned. "I don't think we'll have to wait long. I already feel that we're very compatible."

"I do, too. Your parents, where do they live?"

"Palos Verdes. My dad is an attorney and Mom is a nurse, an R.N. I'd like for you to meet them. They're good people."

Dakota was surprised he wanted her to meet his parents so soon. The idea was a bit scary, but she didn't think warming up to it would be a problem. "Which of your parents do you look like?"

"People say I'm a combination of both. My grandmother used to say I had my mother's smile and my dad's dark eyes. Majority of folks say my dad spat me out."

"What do you think?"

"I think both parents contributed to my looks. The older I get, the more I look like my father. Both of them are beautiful people, inside and out. Do you favor either or both of your parents?"

"Definitely my mother. Same complexion, hair and eye color," Dakota said.

"By the way, you didn't ask me my favorite color. It's the same as your eyes."

"Hazel?" Dakota laughed. "What do you own that's hazel?"

Ethan shrugged. "I didn't say I owned anything. I merely said your eyes are my favorite color." He snapped his fingers. "I do have a hazel sweater. You want to see it?"

"I'll take your word," she said jovially.

"Does that mean you don't want to see the bedrooms?"

"Who said that?"

"That's where my hazel sweater is."

Dakota and Ethan laughed.

Ethan got to his feet and then helped Dakota to hers. Taking her by the hand, he walked her toward the back of the large one-story structure, opening the first door he came to. "This is one of two guest rooms." The room was very male/sports-orientated. Lots of posters of football, basketball and baseball memorabilia hung on the walls.

"Why four twin beds? They're so long, longer than a standard twin."

"I have guy friends who wouldn't dare sleep in the same bed. And I don't let my friends drive if they've had too much to drink. We have fraternity meetings at our houses and also take turns hosting sports nights and poker games. We call it the crash room."

Dakota nodded. "Good name for it. Are there boys-only nights?"

"Maria, Mandy and Charlene love sports. Mandy's the only poker player. Let me say this. The ladies are welcome, but they don't come to everything. The frat meetings are for the brothers only, but we host a lot of social events the ladies love to attend."

Ethan's bedroom wasn't as manly as Dakota had thought it would be. It was beautifully decorated and furnished. The huge mahogany sleigh bed and nightstands took up nearly an entire wall. The fireplace could be seen from anywhere in the room. Two wingback chairs, with a round dark hardwood table in between, were positioned by a paned window. Dakota imagined Ethan sitting there reading or just gazing out the window. His space fit him pretty well: serene, comfortable and charming.

Ethan guided her over to the other side of the room, where he flipped on a light switch and pushed back sliding glass doors. "This is a small terrace, but it gives a lot of serenity. It's dark out so you can't see much, but there's a dense forest beyond the perimeter. I love to hear the birds sing and watch them fly from tree to tree."

Dakota smiled softly. "This is a lovely room, Ethan. I'll think of you in your surroundings when we're apart."

His eyes softened. "Now that's a nice thought."

Ethan gave Dakota a tour of the master bath, with its double sinks and fine wood cabinets, granite counters, Jacuzzi tub, glass shower stall and massive walk-in closet.

Telling Dakota he'd be right back, Ethan disappeared into the deep closet. When he came out, he had on the sweater he'd mentioned earlier. "Don't you think it kind of matches your eyes?"

Dakota didn't think it was even close to her eye color, but he'd never know it. "I see what you mean. I like the sweater."

"Yeah, right!" Ethan snickered. "Seeing your eyes and the sweater at the same time shows me I was way off the mark. But who cares? I still love your hazel eyes."

The information passing between Ethan and Dakota allowed the couple to get to know each other a little better, but he knew they definitely had a ways to go. He wished she was more forthcoming without any prompting from him. Although he had shared some of his family history, she hadn't gotten into hers. He knew her parents were deceased, but she hadn't shared a single detail of their demise. Ethan hoped the day would come when she'd feel comfortable enough with him to open up completely.

Back in the kitchen, without asking Ethan if he wanted help, Dakota began clearing the table, carrying the dishes over to the sink, where she rinsed them off, stacking the dishwasher afterward. He hadn't objected to her help because he liked having her as a team player.

Unable to keep his thoughts inside, Ethan walked up behind and put his arms around her. His nose gently nudged the back of her neck. "I sense a deep reluctance in you to talk in-depth about your life. I've tried not pushing the issue, but I'm interested. I really want to know everything about you, but I'm willing to give it more time."

She wiggled around to face him, running her fingers through his hair. "I'm trying, Ethan. Honest, I am. Every confidant I've ever had has betrayed me in some way. If I don't share my secrets, I don't have to worry about someone using them against me."

"It's easy to see that the death of your parents still affects you." She hadn't mentioned if she had siblings or not. Because of what she'd just said, he felt it'd be intrusive to ask. "Deep pain is often so clear in your eyes. You're dealing with major traumas, but I can't help you cope if you don't trust me. Share your burdens with me."

"Again, I'm trying. This isn't about trusting you. Trusting me is more like it."

"I'm getting it. The woman who emerged at the skating rink and the pizzeria is who I think you are, or at least, the woman you want to be. Keep letting your hair down. You gave us a beautiful experience. Everyone was mesmerized by *that* Dakota."

Dakota swallowed the huge lump in her throat.

Once the couple had settled down on the leather sofa in the family room, Ethan lifted Dakota's right foot and removed her shoe. When she didn't offer any resistance, he tended to the left one. After taking off his shoes, he lodged a throw pillow comfortably behind her head. With his back nestled in one corner of the sofa, he stretched his legs atop the round leather hassock.

Soft piano ballads drifted from the speakers located on each side of the stereo cabinet, which also housed a second plasma television. The recessed lights were kept on dim, but votive candles also burned in the room. He wanted the setting to be romantic.

Surprising Ethan, Dakota laid her head against his chest and closed her eyes. As the sweet music swept into her soul, she felt a yearning for his kiss and tender touch. She wasn't going to battle against offering him her mouth to taste; that's exactly what she desired. They weren't at her front door and she could bet there'd be no brief farewell kiss like all the times before. She wanted to be sure she could finish whatever she started. She liked him, thought he was a great guy. So much good was in his favor.

It was easy to recall how a broken heart felt. It was time to experience a healing.

Regaining her attention, his fingers tenderly stroked her arm. "Tired?"

Wishing he'd pick up on her desire to be kissed, she shook her head. "No."

Visions of him and her wrapped in each other's arms kept her brain in a tizzy. She vividly recalled how the farewell kiss a few nights ago had suddenly deepened. She also remembered how she'd bid him a hasty goodnight.

While Ethan's hand continued to stroke her arm, the fingers on his other one entwined in her hair, twisting it round and round. He liked the satiny feel of her hair, not to mention the sensuous smell of her perfume. A tantalizing gardenia and jasmine scent, he guessed, inhaling deeply, exhaling slowly.

Ethan's desire to take possession of Dakota's tempting mouth was almost more than he could bear. Just the thought of kissing her, their tongues connecting in passion, made his manhood harden.

Dakota's tongue nervously swiped at her lower lip. Her palms felt sweaty, her heartbeat thundering in her ears, as her heart rate continued to hammer away. As his breath suddenly fanned her lips, she shut her eyes and squeezed them tightly. The anticipation of their mouths fully connecting had her nerves clanging like cymbals.

"May I kiss you? Let me kiss you." His voice was husky with desire and his sweet breath softly swept her skin.

Dakota tilted her chin upward. "I want you to kiss me. Please kiss me, Ethan."

It was like she had nearly demanded a kiss. Dakota felt embarrassed, wishing she had quieted her desires.

Ethan no longer held back the potent fervor marching through his body like a unit of storm troopers. Holding back the untamed urgency was impossible. Acting upon his fervent needs, he first kissed her lightly, then passionately, settling her head back against his chest. "Kissing you is incredible," he whispered, his tone laced with longing. "Don't worry about us moving too fast. We've got all the time in the world."

Feeling Ethan's sexual ardor right down to her toes, Dakota's body rode the same surging wave. She was thrilled he hadn't felt her reluctance to dive off the highest cliff without a parachute. She had trusted him. That much was clear.

Dakota felt she was finally ready to hope again. She was soaring high.

Admitting to herself that she'd become a very lonely heart wasn't too hard for Dakota. Until now, her heart was emptier than it had ever been. There'd been no romance and excitement in her life for quite some time. She had missed it desperately. She wanted to welcome Ethan's heated passion with open arms and she didn't want fear to continue playing a major role in the uncertainty. Hoping his patience wouldn't run out too easily, and that they'd continue at a comfortable pace, she closed her eyes, sighing softly.

After slipping quietly into her apartment, Dakota didn't bother to turn on the lights up front. The nightstand lamp was always left on in her bedroom when she hadn't planned to return home until after dusk.

The wattage from the lightbulb was high enough to splash its radiance out into the hallway.

As Dakota dropped down on the sofa, tears had already filled her eyes. She let her pent-up anguish flow unchecked. Her emotions were mixed up again. She'd had a wonderful time at Ethan's, had enjoyed every touch and kiss he'd given her. The deep fear of the betrayed becoming the betrayer was an issue for her, a real stumbling block. Betrayal was a hard emotional ordeal for anyone to recover from.

Continuing to see Ethan without sharing all the details of her life was betrayal?

Craving Ethan's intimate touch was something brand-new for Dakota. This wild sensation flaring in the pit of her womanhood was sweet and hot and overwhelmingly delicious. Ethan's touch was incomparable. Her body responded to him hungrily every time they were in close proximity.

Dakota took into consideration how this was a perfectly normal reaction between a man and woman wildly attracted to each other. He burned for her, too. She felt it every time he touched her. The pulsations in his fingertips, whenever he tenderly stroked her arms, let her feel his emotional and physical status.

The phone startled Dakota. She stared at it like it was an archenemy. Refusing to even look at the caller ID, she got up and quickly walked out of the room. By the time she got down the hall, she found herself rushing over to the phone on her nightstand, praying the call wasn't anything to do with Danielle.

At the same time she glanced at the name and number of the caller, Dakota picked up the receiver. "Ethan," she breathed raggedly, "are you okay?"

"That's what I called to ask you. I'm fine. How did I blow it with you tonight?"

A solitary tear fell from the corner of Dakota's right eye. High anxiety tampered with her stability. "This isn't about anything you've done. I've been a vulnerable soul for a long time. I don't think I can give what you need from me."

"What is it you believe I need from you?"

If Dakota answered the question honestly, she risked exposing the likely unfair assumptions she'd already made about what Ethan needed and desired. "I don't know." Her response was an easier one than what she had once thought.

"Then let me tell you. First off, your friendship is incredibly important to me. I apologize if I've moved too fast for you. I told you earlier we had all the time in the world. I meant that. I wish you could believe me."

"It's not you," Dakota explained. "It's me. I need to sit back and take a full assessment of my life. Haven't done that in a while. Meeting you was sheer coincidence."

"Or sheer fate? What if destiny is calling?"

Tears welled in her eyes. "Oh, Ethan, right now I can't give you the answers. Can I have a little time off to try to think this all through? There's so much we don't know about each other." *The problem is what you don't know about me.*

"How do we get to these things if we don't continue communicating?"

"Good question. Can you believe me if I say I'll call you in a couple of days?"

He sighed heavily. "Why so long, Dakota?"

"I thought we had all the time in the world," she teased.

"Okay, I'll wait for your call. Good night, Dakota."

"Good night, Ethan."

Was destiny truly calling them? Dakota mentally questioned. Destiny sounded nice. Perhaps it may even lead them to paradise. Perhaps.

CHAPTER 4

After closing the brown folder with the lecture outline he'd just delivered inside, Ethan peered out at the tiered seating occupied by the group of young men and women who showed up several times a week to hear what he had to say whether they wanted to or not. Some of them appeared studious, while others looked as if they'd rather be anywhere other than in this room. Many of the guys were unshaven, looking mangy. He easily guessed that a few of his students had major hangovers.

Most of the females came off sophisticated, just the opposite of their immature counterparts. They looked polished, dressed fashionably superb, more often than not. He guessed the head-to-toe matching outfits cost their parents a small fortune.

Ethan couldn't keep from smiling when his eyes quickly raked over Callie Wilkes, Gloria Sadler and Mykala Robards, freshman girls who sat together on the bottom row. They liked giving him a bird's-eye view regardless of the personal disinterest he showed.

These three young ladies came on to Ethan every chance they got, flirting wildly and constantly asking him out. These eighteen-year-olds weren't even legal. He was dead set against dating anyone under the age of twenty-one. It wasn't his thing. Besides, they were still babies in many ways. He wasn't the least bit interested in an affair with a single one of them. And they certainly weren't ready for a mature man like him. Regardless of Ethan's own dating policies, the university did not allow professors to date their current students anyway.

Following behind his last thought, Ethan's next one had him thinking about the call from Dakota. He didn't know if they'd see each other this evening, but he sure hoped so. She had said she'd get back to him with an answer as soon as possible. A couple of days had passed since he'd last seen her, long, lonely ones. He couldn't count the number of times he'd picked up the phone only to put it back down.

As soon as the lecture room emptied, Ethan sighed happily, making his way to the professors' lounge for a hot cup of java.

■ ■ ■ ■

Cleveland Charles summoned Ethan over to his table as soon as Ethan finished pouring coffee into his personalized ceramic mug. Smiling broadly, Ethan sauntered over to the corner table. He sat down with his longtime colleague and friend, greeting the older man cheerfully. "What've you been up to, man?"

"Not a whole lot," Cleveland droned. "How's it been for you?"

"Cool." Honestly, Ethan thought, biting back a few expletives. *It was awful for him without Dakota.* "You're looking kind of down. Are you feeling okay?"

Cleveland palmed his forehead. "Ethan, I've been married twenty-two years. Last week my wife asked me for a divorce, informing me she's in love with a much younger guy. Our son is only eight or nine years younger than the guy she's gaga over. Can you imagine the hurt?"

Ethan realized his dilemma wasn't nearly as bad as Cleveland's, but he couldn't give a discount on his pain. He hurt for the company of Dakota just as much as Cleveland probably wished he could turn back the hands of time. Usually it was the guy who left the wife for the younger, sexier woman. Life *wasn't* fair. His parents had told him that. "I'm sorry, man."

"Ethan, you are like me, one of the decent guys. I have a couple of tickets for the Raiders' game. How about flying up to Oakland with me this weekend?"

Ethan loved the Raiders. With Cleveland feeling so down, he thought he should agree to go, show some humanity. His friend needed a pal right now and so did he. "Who're they playing?"

"The Steelers."

"I'm in. I love both teams." Ethan got to his feet. "Call me this evening with the details. I'm usually home after seven."

Cleveland looked mighty pleased. Ethan was glad for the distraction.

Dakota stared at the phone. It had been a couple of days since her last conversation with Ethan. She still hadn't made a decision to see him this evening, but her heart was closer to winning the battle than her head was. She'd done a lot of soul searching over the past couple of days.

Wishing she had been more honest about her life with Ethan wasn't going to change things. She'd missed out on great opportunities to open up to him. How many times and in how many ways had he asked her to just share with him?

Dakota felt she had too much baggage along for this ride, which was in fact quite a heavy load. When she thought about all the people she loved and had lost, she knew what was at the very heart of her fears. Even those who'd betrayed her were profound losses because they were no longer in her life. She had believed in their friendships only to find out she'd been in these relationships all alone.

Not knowing how Ethan might react to her unconditional love, commitment and duty to her sweet Danielle also owned a fair share of her fear, a part of what had Dakota keeping him at bay. She had never cared one way or the other what any man thought about it before now.

If the man Dakota got romantically involved with didn't accept her baby sister as a part of her life, they just couldn't stay together. She and Danielle were co-hearts and cohorts, a signed-and-sealed package deal.

It would be no different if Dakota had given actual birth to a baby. She had high expectations, too, and she'd require the man who professed to love her to also respect and accept a child of her own, without

reservation. Danielle wasn't her child bio-
logically, but there was no difference in how
deeply she felt than from any other natural
mother.

Maybe she wasn't being fair by not pre-
senting her situation to Ethan and just let
the chips fall where they may. Dakota felt in
her heart that Ethan was worth the risk. She
couldn't imagine his showing any disdain
for her situation.

Did Ethan fit the bill?

There was one other major obstacle in her
life, but it was the most serious of all.

Everyone had personal secrets and so did
she — deep-seated ones, ones that would
be hard to communicate to a lover. Some
things you just didn't impart, period, in
strict confidence or otherwise.

Making money by working phone-sex
lines wasn't exactly an upstanding career
choice, Dakota knew, but the money paid
her rent, her tuition and kept her afloat.
Most important, the paychecks helped her
to meet Danielle's needs.

It was time for this pity party to be over,
Dakota decided. Dwelling on these matters
wasn't helping. She had more important
things to do, like calling Ethan to say they
were on for this evening.

Grocery shopping was high on Dakota's

list. She was out of practically everything she used. One or two more squeezes of the toothpaste tube would leave it empty. Two more swigs of mouthwash would have the same outcome. The last of the shampoo was used over a week ago, which meant she hadn't washed her hair since . . . and it desperately needed a good grooming. Enough money to go to the beauty shop regularly would be nice, but she used her money for far more important things.

Realizing she'd gotten right back into the pity game, Dakota ran into the bedroom and grabbed her purse. She had to clear her head.

Dakota's cart literally collided with another one. It was her fault because she hadn't been paying close attention to the other traffic in the store.

As Dakota looked up at the person she'd run into, an apology on her lips, she realized she had run smack-dab into Ethan's cart, whose basket was nearly filled to the brim. This couldn't be happening.

Ethan stopped dead in his tracks, drinking in the lovely sight of Dakota, as if she was a tall, cool beverage to ease his thirst on a sweltering summer day. He opened his mouth to greet her, but nothing came out.

This was the first time he'd ever been rendered speechless.

"Hello, Ethan," Dakota said as softly as a whispering breeze. She couldn't believe he stood right in front of her, yet he did. He looked wonderful, but she could see a slight shadowing beneath his eyes. *Was he as restless as she?* "How are you?"

Ethan's hand reached out for hers, tucking it snugly away within his. "At this moment I'm ecstatic. I feel like a prayer was just answered."

This moment was both awkward and thrilling for Dakota. It hadn't been too long ago that she'd made up her mind to see Ethan later. As usual, he was dressed impeccably. He looked the consummate professional. The sports jacket, shirt, tie and leather shoes he wore all complemented each other. He didn't look like a stuffy professor or a nutty one either. He looked good enough to feast off.

Afraid to let go of Dakota's hand, Ethan grasped it tighter. "Think we can slide over to the Starbucks inside the store? I'd love to sit down and chat for a few minutes. Seems like an eternity since we've last seen each other."

Dakota quietly admitted to herself she'd really missed him. "I'd like that."

Ethan quickly untangled their carts and then walked by her side to the coffee shop. Upon arrival, the couple quickly found a cozy table where no one could hear their conversation. He had to know where he stood.

Ethan wasted no time in ordering two coffees and the pastry Dakota had requested.

By the time Ethan returned to Dakota, his nerves twanged with thoughts of what to say to her. A lot of emotional stuff coursed through him, for this was the first time he realized he was angry at her for locking him out of her life. Yet he didn't want to come off as an injured party. It wouldn't work well for either of them.

"I can't believe we shop at the same grocers," she said, hoping to break the ice with something less complicated than what they both obviously felt. "This is my favorite place to buy food. I come here twice a month. There's a smaller grocery store closer to my house. I'm constantly in and out of there for spur-of-the-moment items."

Ethan suddenly slammed the side of his fist down on the table, startling Dakota. "Grocers isn't what I want to discuss. I want to talk about *us*. Why didn't you call me back and where do we stand? That's what I want to know." He knew he'd failed at keeping his anger at bay, but he needed answers.

It was hard for Dakota to calm the quivering in her stomach. She knew his outburst was passionate aggravation more than plain anger. "I planned to call you when I got back home from the store. I'm sorry I didn't do it right away."

"I accept," he said hurriedly, impatient to move on to the main issues.

The stress in his voice put Dakota on edge.

"This is already complicated for me, but I don't want it to be. I stayed away because my fears are larger than I thought. I don't know how to conquer them. Nor do I know where we stand or where we go from here."

"Complicated isn't how this has to be for us, Dakota. We were off to a nice start. We've had a little over a dozen dates, each one of them great. I don't want to see us give up on an awesome journey. It's not often two people hit it off as famously as we have. I want to get to know you and you me. I really meant that."

His seemingly sincere remarks were deeply felt by Dakota. Still, she had to wonder. If it wasn't overly complicated now, it was mainly because sex wasn't involved. If and when that happened, the odds of their relationship not becoming convoluted weren't good.

"Listen, we can work this out," Ethan continued. "What if we don't do exclusive right now and give ourselves more time to work up to that? I realize I rushed you on it over dinner that night. If you want to see other people, okay, but I don't want to know about it or discuss it." Ethan ran his hands over his hair. "Guys don't ask for much, do we? We never do."

Dakota suddenly teared up, then straightened and looked Ethan dead in the eye. "About your earlier question of us seeing each other, want to come over and help me fix dinner later on?"

Keeping himself from grinning like a Cheshire cat was just impossible. "I'd love to. Thanks."

Looking over at her basket, Dakota quickly scanned its contents. "Have you ever tried flat-iron steak?"

"I can't say I have. What is it?"

"A very tender cut of beef, extremely easy to prepare," she explained, her eyes aglow with unspent moisture. "Do you like squash?"

"All kinds, but my favorite is the summer variety, the yellow one."

"Mine, too." She smiled.

"See, that's one more thing we have in

common," Ethan remarked.

"It is, isn't it?" She drained her coffee cup and then quickly wrapped a napkin around the leftover pastry. "We should finish shopping now so we both can get back home. I need to prepare."

She got to her feet and threw away her trash. Nervous, she focused on fumbling through her purse. She glanced at her watch. "Is seven-thirty okay with you?"

"Works perfectly. Would you like me to wait and help you carry out your bags?"

"Thanks, but I can manage."

Leaning into her, Ethan kissed her lips gently. "I can't wait to see you."

Dakota blushed. "Me neither," she said, daring to kiss him back.

Ethan expected this evening to be an extremely interesting one. As he watched her walk away, pushing her cart, he laughed within. This was one more date with her he was looking forward to. Spending more time with her was what he'd fervently prayed for all week long. "Let the evening begin."

Dakota's earlier trepidations had been put to rest by the time she reached home. She stepped back into her residence and hurried into the kitchen, where she put away the items she didn't plan to use right away. The thought of sharing the cooking duties with Ethan excited her. She was sure they'd have a lot of fun. She was grateful that she'd been taught to cook. Ethan might be surprised by how good she was in the kitchen. No matter what happened between them, she welcomed the euphoria she felt over spending the entire evening in his company.

The heather-gray linen slacks Dakota chose to wear for her date with Ethan were a perfect fit. Matching the pants with a Christmas-red sweater with a V neckline was a good choice. The simple diamond solitaire pendant, her late mother's, beautifully accessorized her slender neck, as did the matching diamond studs gracing her small earlobes. She only wore this particular set of jewelry on special occasions. This unexpected date with Ethan definitely qualified as exceptional.

The phone rang at the same time Dakota walked back into the kitchen. She quickly picked up the extension, propping herself on the nearby stool.

"Dakota, this is Tallia," said the commanding voice. "We just had someone call in sick this evening. I know you worked earlier, but can you fill in on this shift?"

"Wish I could, but I'm afraid I can't. I've already made plans. I'm sorry."

"Me, too," came the curt reply.

Then the phone line went dead.

Proud of how she'd handled the short-lived conversation with one tough manager, Tallia Norton, Dakota went about her tasks, humming softly.

As Dakota gave more thought to the call, she realized how much out of her character her reaction had been. The firmness in her tone was also unusual for those who knew her. She wouldn't go as far as to call herself a pushover, but she did let the Licensed to Thrill management shove her around more than she should. Normally, she would've gone in to work, without giving it any thought. She'd miss the extra money on her next paycheck, but cash wasn't everything. *Well, that wasn't true in her case.* Still, Dakota was pleased by how things had played out. Saying no wasn't so bad.

Ethan closely examined the flat-iron steak, holding it under the running water in the kitchen sink. It was a good-looking cut of beef, tender but firm to the touch. "So this is what you refer to as flat-iron steak. I still can't wait to taste it."

Dakota smiled knowingly. "I promise it

won't be the last time you'll eat it. It'll more than likely become a regular stock item in your fridge. The spices I use on it are right there," she said, pointing out the row of plastic containers. "Just sprinkle on and rub in a little of everything. I sprinkled the baked potatoes with the same spices."

"I got it covered. How're you preparing the squash?"

"I'd planned to steam it. Would you like it cooked some other way?"

Ethan nodded. "Steaming is fine. I like it sautéed with butter and slices of onion. I also munch on it raw."

"I have onions and butter. Let's try it your way. You can help guide me."

All movement came to a sudden halt as Ethan's eyes connected soulfully with hers. He took this perfect opportunity to kiss her deeply, his tongue teasing her lower lip. "I'm the perfect guide, sweetheart. I do it so well."

There was sudden fiery heat pulsating through Dakota, making her hot and bothered. She just bet he could *do it* well.

Gently taking out of Dakota's hand the knife and peeled brown onion, Ethan held the pungent-smelling vegetable firmly onto the cutting board. He then showcased his adeptness in slicing, dicing and mincing food items. "My father taught me how to cut up things without making my fingers a part of the meal. I also used to be in charge of cutting up veggies for the salad bar in a local restaurant during my college days."

"You sure know how to handle a knife," Dakota praised.

He wiggled his eyebrows. "That's not all I know how to handle, baby."

Dakota giggled at his corny joke.

The meal was soon ready and they sat down to eat. Closing his eyes, Ethan savored the slice of beef he slowly chewed on. It was beyond tender and he loved the delicious taste. "I'm sold on this flat-iron, kiddo. Thanks for the introduction. It'll be on hand in my freezer."

Dakota beamed at him. "Won't say I told you so, but I'm glad I did. As for freezing it, I never do. I somehow fear that'll ruin it. I only buy the meat the same day I cook it. Dan . . ." Unable to keep eye contact with him because of her verbal fumble, she rapidly looked down into her plate. She had nearly said Danielle loved the steak as much as she did.

Dan, he mused. *Who the hell is Dan? Is he the jerk responsible for her personal fears?* Probably so, he concluded, after thinking about how quickly she'd looked away from him. Move on, he thought. She had been hurt. He had to turn a deaf ear on what she'd said, despite the fact she'd called out another man's name, but it wouldn't keep him from wondering about this Dan person.

Almost as if fate had a way of showing up at opportune times, Ethan's cell phone rang. He was glad for the diversion, though he'd thought he had turned it off. It was rude to have it ringing when on a date. Nobody but the person he was with should earn that much importance. He didn't recognize the number on the screen, but he didn't care. The timing was too perfect to bother with second-guessing it.

"Hey, Ethan, sorry to call your cell, but you didn't answer your home phone. It's way after seven," Cleveland said. "Are you in a position to write down some information?" He looked around for something to write on, quickly spotting the message pad on the counter.

As Ethan reconnected his gaze with Dakota, he took note of her questioning look. "Can I use the message pad over there?" He pointed out its location.

Swiftly, Dakota got up from the table and ran over to pick up the bright pink pad. Carrying it back to the table, she handed it to Ethan.

Holding up one finger, Ethan signaled to Dakota he'd only be a minute.

Curiosity shimmered in Dakota's eyes as she closely studied Ethan, wondering exactly what he was jotting down.

Ethan smiled brightly. "I'll see you at LAX early Saturday evening. I'm looking forward to the quick getaway. Can hardly wait for Sunday to roll around."

That tidbit of information signaled an overnight stay to Dakota. Well, since he was flying to his destination, it made sense he'd stay overnight. There'd been no mention of his return date.

A weekend getaway? Where and with whom? She had to wonder.

Dakota absolutely had the feeling Ethan wasn't talking to a woman, but she wasn't positive. No matter if someone tried to hide it or not, there was an altogether different way folks communicated when talking to the opposite sex. Nothing intimate had to be going on either. It was just an act of nature when different genders conversed. Men normally had a way of talking low and sweet to females. Women also had a certain style of talking to men and neither were they above playing the flirting game.

How well Dakota knew about all of that.

Ethan turned off his cell and latched it

back into the holder on his belt. "Sorry about that, lady. I don't normally leave this thing on when I'm on a date, especially during one of the best home-cooked meals I've had lately. The information I got was important to the mission or I would've called back later."

Dakota looked perplexed. *The mission?* Interesting choice of words he'd uttered, she thought. The comments he'd made had actually left things open to interpretation. It could also be seen as an invitation for someone to be downright nosy, anyone other than her, that is. She laughed inwardly at her curiosity.

CHAPTER 5

Ready to clear the table in order to serve dessert, Dakota got to her feet. She had cheated on that part of the meal. Instead of whipping up something herself, she had baked a frozen Mrs. Smith's apple pie. It probably tasted more delicious than anything she could've produced with her own two hands.

The same as Dakota had done when Ethan had prepared dinner for her at his place, he got up and pitched right in with the kitchen chores. Much to her pleasure because she still felt so full, he had also decided to wait on dessert. Like hers, his stomach was filled to capacity.

Ethan rinsed out the dish towel before hanging it up on the rack to dry. "My father used to say we should never complain about doing dishes because it meant somebody ate. Everyone isn't so fortunate to sit down to the abundant meals we have three times

117

a day, not including snacks. He often gave us little nuggets of his wisdom."

Dakota nodded her understanding. "Daddy told us to never balk at going to work, mentioning how many men would love to have a job to go to, to be able to take care of their families half as good as what God had afforded him."

"Some of us just don't realize how blessed we are. God has shone His favor on me and I never hesitate to tell my students my point of view. There's a line I have to be careful to cross when spirituality comes into play, but I still get my points across without getting into hot water," Ethan articulated.

Dakota was so conflicted about many things to do with God. Not about Him, but about how she handled what she knew to be good and right. It wasn't always possible to do the right thing. At least, that's what she told herself to try to justify some of her bad deeds, like working where she did.

Ethan glanced at his watch. He'd been there four hours. He could hardly believe it, but this was what happened when they got together. Time flew as they thoroughly enjoyed each other. To make sure there'd be a next time, he got to his feet. "Walk me to the door?"

Dakota successfully hid how stunned she

was at Ethan's decision to leave her home this early. *Had she unwittingly done something to run him off?* No, she hadn't done a thing, she easily concluded. Instead of protesting her dismay at his leaving, she stood and took a hold of his hand. "Thanks for coming. I had a wonderful time. I'm glad you loved the flat-iron steak."

Ethan tenderly squeezed her hand. "Thanks for having me over. The pleasure was immense. I'd like to cook the steak next time. Cool with you?"

Dakota smiled brightly. "Cool. Let me know when." She knew it wouldn't be on Saturday or Sunday. He was leaving town, off to only God knew where.

At the front door Ethan kissed Dakota passionately. "Hey, because I'm flying up to Oakland Saturday for the Raiders' game on Sunday afternoon, how about getting together Friday night with my friends and me for bowling? Is that a possibility?"

"Most definitely." Had he read her mind? The thought of his going away had stayed on her mind from the first mention of an airport meeting. Now that she knew his plans, she felt better, but she still didn't know who his companion was. *Would knowing the answer make her feel a million times better or a trillion times worse?*

"One of my colleagues has tickets for the football game and invited me along. Cleveland's an older guy who loves to give us young guys good advice. He's almost like a father figure. I don't go out with him socially, but we talk at work a lot during breaks." Placing his hands tenderly on both sides of her face, he looked into her eyes. "I'll miss you until I see you again. Think you'll miss me, too?"

Dakota placed her hands over his, nesting her face more snugly between his gentle hands. "I'm sure of it." She looked down at the floor. "Kind of having a hard time believing the evening has come to an end so abruptly. But it's been really nice."

Surprised by her comment, he raised an eyebrow. Although it halfway sounded like an invitation for him to stay longer, he would leave. He wanted to make sure she had enough space to breathe.

The look of surprise in Ethan's eyes wasn't lost on Dakota. Wanting to make sure he left her home knowing she definitely wanted him to come back again and again, she pressed her lips into his for a fleeting kiss. His hands dropped from her face and his arms immediately wrapped around her in a tight embrace. Lifting her off her feet, he returned the kiss, his tongue locking with hers. He stood her back on her feet. "Good night. Call you tomorrow about Friday."

"Sounds like a plan. Tomorrow, Ethan."

Almost as restless as he'd been during the times there'd been no communication with Dakota, Ethan paced his bedroom floor. It was too late to go hang out with his friends, yet still too early to go to bed. He had an idea he wouldn't sleep any better than he had on the nights of their separation. For the umpteenth time he asked himself why he hadn't stayed at her place after he'd gotten the impression she had wanted him to.

Trying to play it safe wasn't getting him anything but another lonely night, not to mention more thoughts about the mystery guy named Dan.

Ethan wished he hadn't thought of what had occurred earlier. Now all he wanted to do was find out who this guy was and what exactly he meant to Dakota.

Walking out of his bedroom and down the hallway, Ethan went into the office and pulled out from the file cabinet the folder. Working on his project would hopefully help take his mind off Dakota, who he already missed something awful.

Inside his retreat, Ethan dropped down on the two-cushion leather couch set. After flipping on the plasma TV, he surfed a few channels. Getting caught up in the commercial running, one he'd seen numerous times, he intently eyed the vivid, lively images filling up the screen. Just as he began mulling over the idea of phoning Dakota, the ring tone on his cell cost him the next thought.

"Hey, Cleveland, what's up?" Ethan had heard a strain in his colleague's greeting, figuring something serious was up. "Is everything okay, man?"

"My life is anything *but* okay." Cleveland sighed wearily. "Looks like I have to bow out of our plans. But I'd still like you to go. If you can find a traveling companion, you're welcome to both tickets. What do you think of the offer?"

"That it's one I can't refuse." Ethan did a quick mental rundown of his friends. "Maxwell, my best friend, would love to fly to see the Raiders play. I'll give him a call and see if he's free. How will I get the tickets?"

"I'll bring them to work with me," Cleveland remarked. "We'll talk then."

Ethan's brow wrinkled. "Mind sharing the reason you can't go?"

"My wife demanded a meeting for us to discuss divvying up assets. I'm trying to remain civil to keep from involving an expensive attorney. In fact, La Donna wants me to use her lawyer. 'Keep it simple,' she had the nerve to say."

Ethan slapped his forehead with an open palm. "Get your own attorney, man. After taking on a lover, she initiates this messy divorce. Now she has the nerve to try to manipulate you even more." There was a pregnant silence on the other end. Ethan momentarily wondered if Cleveland was still on board. Then he heard breathing.

"Let me be honest here. She's not entirely to blame. I cheated on the marriage first, four years ago." Cleveland mentioned the name of a beautiful and popular female professor at the university. "We were lovers for nearly two years. I actually told my wife I was in love with Sarah. That nearly killed her."

Cleveland's revelation rocked Ethan. Never in a million years would he have guessed at this or ever connect these two people in the same breath, especially as lovers. They were opposites in every way possible. Opposites attract wasn't a theory Ethan readily embraced. For a relationship to work, he thought two people had to have a lot in common. *Could opposites really claim that?* He didn't believe so.

"You *weren't* in love with your mistress?"

Ethan asked.

Cleveland sighed hard. "In lust, the worst kind. What I got myself into would make a man borrow, steal and possibly kill to keep the relationship intact. If I was ever threatened with it ending, I would've lost my mind. It was a wild time for me."

"Sounds like it." Ethan speculated on why Cleveland had chosen him to dump all this garbage onto. They'd known each other for years and had talked plenty, but nothing this personal had ever come up. Cleveland loved to talk about his career. It felt kind of weird becoming the confidant of a man twenty-plus years his senior.

After Ethan and Cleveland spoke a few more minutes about the game, the two colleagues hung up.

Ethan still hadn't found anyone to replace the fun guy who actually owned the Raider tickets. Maxwell turning down the invite had nearly left him speechless. His best friend ate and slept football, but he was spending the weekend at his girlfriend's parents' home in beautiful Montecito.

Just imagining the reaction to Maxwell calling off the cozy family gathering had kept Ethan from pushing any harder. Knowing how high-strung and temperamental

Charlene could get, a cancellation would cause Maxwell to suffer unbearably through her periodic mood swings. Still, she was the perfect woman for Maxwell.

Ethan considered Dakota. To ask her to accompany him to Oakland might cross another line she wasn't ready to step over.

Envisioning him and Dakota flying through the friendly skies together was scintillating. It'd be a relatively short flight to Oakland from LAX, approximately forty-five minutes of air time. He'd have to get a hotel room. Or perhaps two rooms. Maybe she'd go for one room with two beds or he could get a two-bedroom suite. Put it to her and let her decide, he thought. Going through this tiring mind burn was ridiculous when he didn't even know if she'd agree to go.

Call and ask her, he quietly told himself, looking at the phone like it was a two-headed demon. It was either yes or no.

Ethan looked at the clock, deciding this situation had to be resolved tonight, regardless of the hour. He didn't have any more time to waste.

The second Ethan heard Dakota's husky sleep-filled voice, regret over waking her assailed him. The sound of her drowsiness was also sensuous. "Sorry to wake you, but I got a problem. I need your help."

"What's a matter?" she asked with concern.

"I'd like you to fly up to Oakland with me Saturday." He hastily gave her the rundown on his quandary. "Separate rooms or same room with separate beds. I was thinking about booking a suite. Is it doable for you?"

Dakota exhaled loudly. Of course it was doable, only if she could kick her fears to the curb. Being up north with Ethan, in a hotel room, no less, was about as scary as things could get for her. It was certainly an intriguing offer, one she'd love to accept if it wasn't for what she thought it might mean. Separate beds, separate rooms, same room and separate beds all spelled out the same thing for her.

Trouble.

Traveling over four hundred miles away from home, sleeping in the same room, or one nearby, with a man she was wildly attracted to, was a recipe for fiery passion and countless other romantic dreams. Coursing through her, prickly as canned heat, were the delectably wicked vibrations she felt whenever she hung out with Ethan. The insane emotions his very presence invoked were so undeniable that she wouldn't bother trying to.

Being with him *and* away from him was pure torture.

"I'll go," she said.

Dakota was totally surprised at how effortlessly her response had come out of her mouth, but she didn't think it was a matter of free will. Maybe destiny *was* working her. Ethan obviously believed in providence. Maybe she should start believing in it, too. It might make things less complicated.

"You'll go?" He sounded as shocked by her response as Dakota did. "That's great! Thanks. I'm excited," he gushed. It sounded like all his words had run together. He'd never in his life acted this crazy and pumped up over a woman. "We'll come up with a game plan when we get together."

Despite the lateness of the hour, Dakota got out of bed and slid back one side of the double closet doors. Looking over the clothes hanging on the racks, she tried to put together a decent wardrobe for the trip up north. She didn't have a lot, but what she had was of good quality. Thanks to the rich folks who donated or put their items on consignment so she could wear nice things.

Dakota groaned loudly. Decent clothing was one thing, but owning a suitcase to pack them in was an altogether different matter. All she owned was a leather backpack. No way would she go on a trip without adequate luggage. She'd be a laughingstock traveling with what she owned. Didn't everyone have at least one suitcase? Apparently not, she conceded, cringing. She didn't.

Opening the top drawer of her chest, Dakota reached under her lingerie and pulled out a checkbook-style wallet designed in faux leather. She quickly opened it and took out the stash of money. She then began counting the bills.

There was more than enough cash to buy a piece of luggage or two. She didn't want to make the purchase from a thrift shop. She deserved brand-new for a change. It was about time to spend a little money on herself. As long as Danielle didn't have to go without, Dakota convinced herself it was okay to make a one-time purchase. Her finances were in halfway decent shape and she still hadn't had to touch the emergency funds.

Just because she didn't have luggage to pack them in, Dakota didn't think she had to wait to set out the clothes she planned to take. With doing just that in mind, she put the money back in the wallet and returned it to its nesting place. It was late, but she was too excited to go back to sleep.

She wondered what it'd be like to fly again. She felt apprehensive because she hadn't been on a plane since she was nine years old. Her parents had taken her to Washington, D.C., to see the White House and other historical landmarks. That had been a lifetime ago, a time in her life when smiling and laughter had come easy.

It was so hard for Dakota to concentrate on her studies. The superb English lecture had been given and she was now in the library studying the notes she'd jotted down. Garrett Aries was a great lecturer, never leaving anyone disappointed. He knew how to grip and then hold the rapt attention of all his students even if her attention was elsewhere today. Neither the bowling date nor trip had even begun, yet she was already conjuring up the kind of quiet but exciting moments she hoped to share with Ethan. It scared her silly but she couldn't be any happier.

Dakota secured her car and made a fast track to the entrance of the bowling alley. Once inside, she scanned the lanes for Ethan and his friends, dismayed when she didn't spot anyone. Momentarily she wondered if she'd come to the wrong place. That wasn't possible, she decided. Strikes & Spares was where he'd told her to meet him.

The hand suddenly covering her eyes felt tender, soft and very familiar. She smiled. "Nice greeting. Now can I please see your handsome face?"

Ethan chuckled. "That, you can do." Before taking his hands away, he kissed the back of Dakota's head, looking her up and down. "One beautiful sight. And you're working those jeans to death."

"To death? That doesn't sound very pleasant."

He turned her around to face him, his big smile allowing her a full view of his beautiful teeth. "Your figure fitting fabulously into those jeans is pleasant enough, all right, extremely delightful." He'd love to give her beautifully rounded backside a few firm squeezes.

Ethan took Dakota by the hand. "Come with me. The gang is way down there." He pointed at the next-to-the-last lane. "I have to warn you. The ladies are out of sorts, looking for revenge. The guys have been on a roll, a hot streak. My boys have won every game out of our past few bowling sessions."

"Hmm. Maybe I can help out the girls. I used to belong to a league." She didn't mention that her league days were back in high school, when all her teenage friends thought the bowling alley was the perfect hangout. But Dakota had possessed mad bowling skills back then. "What did you bowl?"

Ethan shrugged. "I haven't. It would've made the teams uneven. The thing to do was to wait until you showed up. The ladies said it wasn't fair for me to bowl."

As Dakota and Ethan walked to the group, they were having a loud, lively discussion. No one seemed to notice their presence. She took a seat to listen to what was being said, wanting to know what was what.

Looking mad as a wet hen, Charlene was accusing the guys of cheating. Dakota didn't know how you could cheat at bowling, but she'd heard Maria say they'd been pencil-whipped. The women were accusing the men of cheating on the scores. She had followed along okay until Maria swiftly broke out in Spanish, directing her seemingly poisonous comments at Rudy, who may've been the only one who understood her. Seconds later, Dakota changed her mind about who knew what.

Ethan obviously understood the foreign language, too, as he jumped in, arguing passionately with Maria in her native language. It appeared that the others at least had some knowledge of Spanish. Dakota was the only one in total darkness.

Maria then switched back to English, just when Dakota began to understand the body language, right as the feud was getting good. The waving of hands and pumping up fists was a strong indicator of the passion each felt about their point of view.

"Can we get back to the game of bowling?" Rudy asked. "We can start all over if you ladies want us to. We didn't cheat," he stated emphatically.

Dakota had laced up her bowling shoes during the arguing. She stepped up to the lane, happy she could help get this party restarted. Picking up the ball, she rubbed it gently for a couple of seconds. Positioning herself like she knew what she was doing, she showed off great form. Then, with a strong swing of her right arm, she let the ball fly.

The shiny bowling ball swayed from side to side. It then began spinning like a top, moving more and more toward the center of the lane. The pins began falling in one fell swoop. Every single one was gone, resulting in a strike. The ladies went wild, jumping up and down, shouting Dakota's name, exchanging high fives among them.

The bowling competition was on again.

Dakota had sparked a winning spirit in the women. They were now ready to annihilate the guys. Each time their turn came, they closely studied the lane, as if it was a fine science. If the females didn't make a strike, they made sure to pick up the spares.

Dakota made strikes on her next three attempts. The two times she didn't strike, she spared, pumping her fists in the air afterward. Like she'd done in her old high school cheerleading days, she cheered on her comrades as they stepped up to the lane. She had a blast, booing loudly when the men were up, earning a few dark glances. Dakota didn't care what the men thought of her. She only cared about the ladies winning it all.

Ethan looked as if he was really proud of Dakota. The gleam in his eyes was for her and he couldn't seem to pull away his gaze. She knew his attention was steadfast on her. His display of affection made her feel good all over.

The losers had agreed to buy dinner for the winners. Hamburgers and French fries was the ladies' choice for dining. Dakota had a taste for fried fish, but she went along with the program. After all, she was a newcomer. In separate cars the group caravanned over to a distant Fanny's Burgers, a popular chain. Because she had driven herself to the bowling alley she had to drive alone to the burger joint. Ethan had followed along right behind her in his car to make sure she was safe.

"Pass the ketchup, please," Maxwell requested of Ethan. The two best friends sat opposite each other at the long table the staff had readied for the group of eight.

Ethan frowned. "I guess you're not planning on kissing Charlene tonight."

Maxwell raised an eyebrow. "Why'd you say that?"

"You only have a mountain of onion rings on your plate. I wouldn't want to kiss you," Ethan announced, cracking up.

"I hope not," Maxwell said, chuckling. "That'd be taking our friendship a bit far."

Everyone but Ethan, who looked rather sheepish, laughed at Maxwell's comical remarks. Ethan knew he'd stepped into that one with both feet.

The waiter showed up with the orders. Everyone grew quiet as the food received all the attention. It smelled heavenly and the group was ravenous and ready to dig in.

Ethan looked at Dakota. "Enjoying yourself?"

"You bet." She consulted her watch. "It's getting late, though. I should go home as soon as we finish eating. I have a few errands to run tomorrow, before our flight."

"Couldn't find time to get it all done today?"

"I didn't have enough time to finish everything. But I promise to get to the airport on time. I won't be late tomorrow."

Ethan looked surprised. "What're you talking about? Don't you want me to pick you up? There's no need for us to pay parking fees for both cars."

Dakota gave a quick shake of her head. "You hadn't mentioned picking me up, so I assumed I needed to get there on my own. In fact, we haven't talked about any trip details. Maybe we should do that now."

A quick glance around the table showed Ethan that no one was paying attention to them. Maxwell was the only one who knew about Oakland, but he hadn't told him Dakota was traveling with him. He knew he'd take a good ribbing over it. She wouldn't be spared either. He didn't want anyone making distasteful jokes about their engaging in a romantic rendezvous. That kind of scenario probably wouldn't go over well with Dakota. She was a private person. Exposing their plans would embarrass her.

135

It was best to keep things strictly between them.

Leaning up against Dakota's car, Ethan reached out and pulled her into his arms. He hugged her warmly, loving the feel of her in his tight circle of strength. The tender way he looked at her made her heart tingle. She had the same effect on him. Just looking at her made his insides flutter uncontrollably. They'd shared yet another beautiful night. Neither of them wanted to see it come to an end.

Dakota knew that she'd soon have Ethan all to herself. Perhaps that would make it easier for her to let him go on his merry little way. They'd already prolonged the evening by his following her home. She didn't want to be lonely tonight, but she would be. Missing him as much as she did always surprised her. Once they parted after this little tryst, she'd probably long for him more than ever before. Being away from him was like a physical hurt, a throbbing toothache.

Holding back on his desire for intimacy wasn't easy for Ethan. Dakota's juicy lips looked as if they were begging for his kisses. He remembered how sweet she tasted. He could never forget the kisses they'd shared because it was all he'd thought about since the very first one.

As Ethan's mouth gently claimed hers, Dakota didn't resist. She welcomed his affection, letting herself go with the flow.

CHAPTER 6

Although the animated film *Shark Tale* had been around a good while, Dakota and Danielle viewed it as often as *Happy Feet*. The array of celebrity voices made the film especially interesting. Danielle never failed to laugh all the way through the film.

Tired and bleary-eyed, Dakota had gone to bed at 1:00 a.m. and had gotten right back up at 4:30 in order to make sure she saw Danielle before she went away. Staying out much later last night with Ethan than she'd planned had required her to stay up late to take care of several important things once she'd made it home.

Making sure all checks were written out for the monthly bills and getting them in the mail had been one of the more important tasks. She had also written the check for Danielle's residence fees, which she paid quarterly. She planned to hand-carry the payment to the business office once it opened up at 8:00 a.m. Dakota had been carrying a heavy load for a long time.

Dakota and Danielle, stretched out on the floor comfortably in sleeping bags, had pillows lodged beneath their heads. Danielle was still in her colorful Dora pajamas and Dakota had nearly fallen back to sleep a couple of times already. Three and a half hours of shut-eye hadn't been nearly enough downtime for someone who normally got in an adequate amount of sleep, especially on workdays.

The siblings had had breakfast already. Scrambled eggs, sausage links, buttermilk biscuits, orange juice and milk and cereal had been consumed with gusto. For such a tiny girl Danielle had a ravenous appetite. Breakfast was the little girl's favorite meal of the day. Pancakes and maple syrup was a favorite treat for her any time of the day. But big sister didn't allow too much of the sweet liquid.

Dakota lightly stroked Danielle's long, thick braids, as they continued to watch the movie. The child's hairdo had been changed on Wednesday. Every week Dakota paid Meryl Walker to come to the residence home and wash and style her sister's hair, though sometimes it had to be neglected when she wasn't feeling well.

Dakota momentarily thought of telling Danielle about her trip out of town, but it worried her that the child might grow anxious over her absence. Since the death of their parents, they were never very far away from each other for extended periods of time. Danielle had fears that Dakota might go away and never come back, just like their parents. She hoped to get back in time for a visit because of it. Whether they attended the facility chapel or stayed in the room for Bible study, it was a special time.

Danielle got up from the sleeping bag and retrieved the checkerboard from a low shelf inside the cabinet. Smiling, she carried the game over to where her sister lay quietly. "I'll win this time, Kota. You won last game." Danielle giggled. "You want to bet?"

Looking surprised, Dakota laughed. "Bet? What do you know about betting?"

Shifting her body until she could reach the nightstand, Danielle opened the top drawer. Reaching inside, she pulled out several small trinkets. "I won these."

Dakota had difficulty believing her eyes. The gifts were small but nice. "Where'd those come from?"

"Nurse Compton. We play lots of games. She can't beat me at checkers. I get a small gift when I win."

"And what does Nurse Connie get when she wins?" Connie Compton was the last person Dakota would've suspected as the trinket bandit. No doubt she meant well, but she probably hadn't given any thought to teaching Danielle a bad habit. It was gambling, no matter how you looked at it.

"Kisses and hugs. She says I give good hugs." Danielle giggled some more. The depth of her excitement clearly showed in the animated way she clapped her hands.

The little girl looked so happy and proud of her prizes. No way could Dakota scold Danielle about anything she'd received from winning. But she would nicely tell the nurse what she feared and why it shouldn't continue.

"I don't have anything to bet you, but I'm going to win," Dakota challenged.

"You got a million hugs and kisses." Danielle smiled sweetly, nearly bringing Dakota to tears. Her charming innocence glowed like a string of stars against the backdrop of a black velvety sky. She knew all about her sister's great hugs and kisses and she couldn't wait until the game was over. Dakota just needed to feel the love right now.

Bracing herself against the fear rising up in

her belly like the force of a hurricane, Dakota held her breath, gripping the ends of the armrests. She watched the color drain from her knuckle as the airplane ascended, flying deeper into the white clouds. Dakota didn't remember that much about the D.C. flight she'd taken with her parents.

Glad that willpower had finally won out over her incredible urge to grab on to Ethan's hand and hold it for dear life, Dakota reached up to her forehead and wiped away the small beads of sweat. As the plane leveled off, she began to settle down.

Allowing Dakota to maintain her dignity, Ethan refrained from addressing her fears and discomfort. Her lovely eyes had reflected sheer terror when the plane had begun its initial ascent. The wild fluttering of her eyelashes had been another indicator of her reaction to the huge hunk of metal soaring right into the ether.

"They'll come around in a minute and offer us something to drink," Ethan told his companion. "They have juices, soft drinks, wine and other alcoholic beverages." She looked as if she could use a straight shot of something strong to help calm her down. "What about a glass of wine?"

"Perfect," she said a tad too quickly. Embarrassed by her quickness of tongue, she pressed her lips together, as if it might keep another telling remark from escaping.

Ethan laughed inwardly. She was so adorable in her state of uncertainty. She looked as if she wondered what in the world she'd gotten into. At one time in his life he had been afraid of flying, too. Frequency in the air had eventually remedied his phobia.

Beverage service attendants came around and Ethan ordered two chardonnays. He didn't know if Dakota had eaten or not. That concerned him. Wine on an empty stomach, coupled with her bad case of nerves, wasn't an ideal mixture.

"Have you eaten?"

She nodded. "Full breakfast with Dan . . ." Her voice trailed off. "Yes, I've eaten."

There was that monstrous name again. Her sentence had broken off just like before, when she'd said it at dinner the other night. Ethan was irritated that she'd have breakfast with another man knowing she was flying away with him later in the afternoon. He suddenly felt jealous.

Why did she agree to a trip to Oakland with him if she had a man waiting in the wings for her? Just imagining her being in the arms of another man had him bristling. Jealousy was a brand-new sensation for him and he didn't like the feel of it.

Ethan's self-confidence had never allowed him to question what another man may or may not have over him. He never worried about anything to do with other men, period. The only man he had ever tried to mimic was his father, one of the best men God had breathed life into. *Was Dan someone he should really worry about?*

The wine was served and it helped take Ethan's mind off what Dan might mean to Dakota. He opened each small bottle and poured the contents into the plastic glasses the flight attendant had provided. Reaching down for his bag, he opened it and searched around inside until he came up with two sandwiches. She had only mentioned eating breakfast, which had occurred a long time ago. The food he provided could help stomach absorption. Ethan didn't want Dakota to get the least bit sick from the wine.

A few minutes later, when the airplane suddenly flew into turbulence, the fasten seat belt signs came on, startling Dakota. Then the captain's deep voice came over the speaker, asking everyone to buckle up and stay seated.

Ethan slipped his arm around Dakota. Right after he'd put his arm around her, he felt the tension in her body ease. Without any prompting from Ethan, Dakota laid her head against his chest. He smelled divine, like always. Feeling safe and secure, she closed her eyes. "I think my nerves are calmer now." She looked up at him and smiled softly. "Or maybe it's your comforting presence. Whatever it is, it makes me feel good."

"That's nice to hear."

Dakota fleetingly touched Ethan's face with the back of her hand. "It's hard for me to believe I'm sitting next to you in an airplane. The flying part is scary, but being here beside you is thrilling."

Dakota's remarks had again caught Ethan off guard. *Was she toying with him? Did she view their relationship as a cat-and-mouse game?* One minute she was scared to death of any intimacy. Then she'd turn right around and stimulate his desire for passion. "You're not alone in that, Dakota. I enjoy every moment we spend together."

Dakota looked out the window, overcome by the impassioned way he sometimes looked at her and into her. His dark, hot gaze felt like it penetrated her body from the inside out, making her flesh feel like melting candle wax.

"Why don't you ever fly anywhere?" Ethan inquired, interrupting her thoughts.

"No reason to. Don't get any opportunities. But I think I can get into it. Maybe I'll do more traveling, depending on how this trip goes."

What Dakota had said to Ethan was the dreamer part of her at work, not her reality. She couldn't just go off and willingly leave Danielle for pleasure. This time away was an exception. Traveling was another reason it was so hard to have a personal relationship. Couples loved to get away together for long weekends and vacations. That wasn't in the cards for her. This short jaunt may leave her craving for more, but she knew how to curb her appetite. She'd done it all her adult life.

The seat belt sign turned on again, followed by the captain's voice. They were on final approach to the Oakland Airport. One of the attendants followed up on the captain's remarks by instructing everyone to turn off and store all electronic devices for the duration of the flight. The use of cell phones would be permitted only after landing.

Inside the airport terminal, Ethan and Dakota hurried to where the rental car agency was located.

Less than thirty minutes later Ethan

directed Dakota onto a shuttle bus that transported passengers to the rental car lot. The couple carefully stored their luggage on metal racks and then claimed seats close to an exit door.

Sighing, Ethan ran his fingers through his hair. "Traveling can be tedious. Flying from city to city was much easier to cope with before 9/11. Now it's a nightmare. Some security procedures are necessary, while others are a waste of time. If all the security measures in place are keeping us safe, I'll happily continue to deal with it. I don't fly nearly as much as I used to."

"I enjoyed the flight after I got my fears under control. Like I said before, I found comfort in being with you. I've already decided I'd like to try flying again. I'll have to take short jaunts, though."

"Why only short trips?" Ethan asked.

"Work, school and not a lot of leisure time."

Danielle counted on Dakota and she wanted and needed to be around whenever the staff called to request her presence. It happened with less frequency. Danielle wasn't depressed as much anymore. It had taken a long time for the sisters to work through the dark depression resulting from the death of their parents. Their grandparents had been there for them and then they'd passed away unexpectedly.

"Do you attend school in the summer, too?" he asked.

"I did this past summer, but I'm not sure I'll do it again. It's hard studying during the summer months when you want to laze around and lay out at the beach. I just wish I hadn't had to wait so long to go back to school. We can't predict the future, so when things happen unexpectedly we have to heed the call. I stepped up to the plate when my parents died. I had no alternative."

This was an opportunity to learn more about the tragedy, but he decided against it. "I get the impression you've had some heavy burdens to carry. I don't want to pry into your personal life, but if you need me, I'm here for you. I can't make it any plainer."

"Heavy burdens, Ethan, yet I feel extremely blessed. Mom and Dad taught me that God puts on us no more than we can bear. I believe it. There is always someone who has a story far more painful and much more devastating than mine. There are many people who have greater needs than me, period."

The Mustang convertible Ethan had rented

was metallic blue with a white top. Dakota knew these were the kinds of cars cops loved to target. For whatever reason, many folks who drove them had a tendency to race at top speeds. She hoped Ethan was an exception to that rule of thumb, but she decided to share her feelings on speed.

"I know some people think convertibles are meant to be driven fast, but fast-moving cars scare me plenty." With her parents dying in an automobile accident, she simply wasn't keen on speed.

He looked over at her for a quick second, curious about her statement. "I promise to stay well within the speed limit. I'm also a careful driver."

The two-bedroom hotel suite was nearly as big as her apartment. Lavishly decorated with ornamental vases of fresh flowers, beautiful works of art and all sorts of lovely candles in intriguing holders, the room had strong character. The Oriental-style furnishings carved from shiny black lacquer were nicely appointed. One bedroom had a king-size bed and the other housed a queen-size bed.

Ethan had dropped off Dakota's new luggage in the larger of the two rooms. He felt the space had been designed with royalty in mind, making her deserving of sleeping there. The suite would've cost him quite a few bucks if he hadn't used his hotel guest points, which he had plenty of. If he'd had to pay for the room, it wouldn't have been a problem. Ethan wanted their experience to be beautiful and so much more.

Upon Dakota's request, Ethan hoisted the suitcase onto the luggage stand and moved aside for her to open it. "I'm going to unpack, too. See you in a few minutes."

Dakota nodded. "Okay. It shouldn't take me long to put away the few things I brought with me." She watched after Ethan as he left the room. She liked how things had gone so far. They were connecting very well.

Dakota was finding it increasingly hard not to mention Danielle in his presence. She'd done it twice that she knew of. *What did Ethan think of how she'd quickly suspended her comments?* Depending on how the weekend turned out, she intended to tell him soon.

Dakota slipped from the bedroom and went out onto the terrace. The panoramic view was stunning. Looking over the city was surreal. How she'd gotten from being terribly fearful, all the way to sharing a hotel suite with Ethan in less than two months was surprising. However, two people very attracted to each other wanted to spend as much time as possible together. To make anything more of it was overcomplicating a simple analogy.

Walking up behind Dakota, Ethan's hands gently circled her waist, clamping together at her midsection. "What do you think of the view?"

Without daring to look back at him, she gulped hard, excited by how his body was so close to hers. "It's spectacular. I've heard so many things about Oakland, but I've never known anyone to say it's a beautiful place to visit."

He rested his chin atop her head. "Like all other major cities, Oakland has a few bad neighborhoods. But it's a lot more than what some people say about it. There are people who love to dwell on the negatives. I'll try to show you what a lot of folks don't get to see."

Ethan turned her around to face him. "Wait until dusk falls. Bright lights bring this city to life. There's a lot of culture and history here. Because we're all through unpacking, do you want to walk around? From what I read on the Internet, the hotel's outdoor gardens are a must-see and the landscaping is breathtaking."

"Would love to. I saw the unbelievable grounds when we drove up. I was hoping I'd get the opportunity to look around."

Ethan tenderly pulled Dakota in closer to his body, kissing first her forehead and then her cheeks and down to her soft lips. His tongue teased hers, slowly darting in and out of her mouth. The sensations skipping through Dakota made her feel light as a feather, as if she might lift off any moment now. Tilting her head back, he sprinkled soft kisses all over her neck and creamy throat. As the fingers on his right hand threaded their way through her silky hair, he inhaled her sweet scent.

If this display of affection was indicative of things to come, Dakota knew her life was about to change. For better or worse.

Holding hands, Ethan and Dakota were in awe of the colorful flower and shrub gardens. The vivid, hearty blooms were plentiful. Fall flowers and colorful mixed foliage ran rampant over the property. Rosebushes, rambling bougainvillea and red, yellow and orange hibiscus flowered in abundance. Tall, sturdy magnolia trees and majestic palms appeared to stand guard over the grounds.

As Dakota and Ethan reached a clearing, a huge crystal-blue lake appeared right before them. Various species of birds randomly took flight, only to land back on the water a few moments later. Dakota felt at peace here. The water was calm, but she saw numerous ripples. Maybe the lake had fish. Their hands linked together felt warm and tender. His attentiveness toward her made her feel alive and special.

As the couple walked on, Ethan gave Dakota a history lesson on Oakland. "During World War II, Oakland was known for ship building. Many people moved to the city for work. In 2001 *Forbes* magazine ranked Oakland in the top ten best places for business and careers. Also, two popular musical groups came out of Oakland in the sixties and seventies. Sly & the Family Stone and Tower of Power."

"That was back in the day for my parents," Dakota said, laughing.

Ethan squeezed Dakota's fingers. "If we get up superearly tomorrow, we can run into San Francisco for a short tour. I'd love to drive you across the Golden Gate Bridge and into Sausalito. It's an awesome experience. We may even get down to Embarcadero Street, which connects Fisherman's Wharf to the Ferry Building. Pier 39 is an amazing outdoor shopping mall. We can't see everything this time, but we can come back again."

"I've seen pictures and postcards of the Golden Gate Bridge, but this'll be my first time to see it. The football game starts at one o'clock tomorrow, so our time is limited."

Ethan smiled at Dakota. "I'm glad you'll experience it for the first time with me. Are you ready to eat something? We can finish the hotel tour after I feed you."

She was touched by his sweet remarks. She'd had so many first-time experiences with him already, each one unique. Building memories with someone special should be fun and she was having a blast. "I could eat just about anything right now. My stomach feels as if it's on empty. The sandwich must've went straight to my feet."

Ethan chuckled. "We'll eat in one of the hotel restaurants. Okay with you?"

Dakota shrugged. "Anywhere you choose is fine."

The decor of the Red Dragon Chinese Restaurant was exquisite. Rich reds, gold and black complements made a bold statement. Colorful Chinese figurines were posted on high ledges all over the restaurant. Dakota was completely taken with the numerous jade carvings and intricate Oriental works of art created on silk canvases.

The menu was very extensive. Sweet and sour chicken was Dakota's choice. Peking duck was appealing to Ethan. Both preferred steamed white rice over fried. Vegetable spring rolls and egg drop or hot and sour soup were part of the combination meals.

In the mood for hot tea, Dakota asked Ethan to pour her a cup. He was only too happy to oblige. He had to wonder if somehow he was going around in circles over her. He wanted to please this woman, wanted to make her feel like a queen — and not a queen for just a day. Not one to fall easy or hard for the opposite sex, Ethan had destroyed his past record. Falling for her had been so easy and profound. Her sweet personality shone with brilliance and that beautiful smile of hers lit up his universe.

"Tell me more about your job, Dakota. You don't mention it much."

"Not a lot to tell, nothing to brag on in telemarketing. It helps pay the bills. School is the most important task for me right now. Education and reinventing me will lead to a better paying job as a teacher. I've wanted to teach since I was a teenager. I believe as a professor, you're providing one of the most important educational services around. Jobs as educators are often thankless ones. But I don't suspect you do it to be thanked."

He smiled. "Thanks. That was a high compliment. And you're right. If anyone is in this business to be shown gratitude, they're in the wrong profession. Educators aren't paid top salaries, but they should be. We're the most underpaid employees around."

"Don't I know it."

"Yet you still want to be an educator."

"Nothing but that, Ethan. I will succeed at it."

"No doubt in my mind. I like your determination." He pushed back from the table. "I'm pretty full right now, but I know I'll be hungry again before long."

"That's the way it is with Chinese food. I know exactly what you're talking about. I'm full, too, but I want to finish my tea. Do you mind if I take out the rest of my food?"

"Of course not."

Ethan immediately summoned the waiter over to pack up the small portions left on her plate. There was a microwave oven in the suite for later warming. There was nothing left of his meal. His parents had never taught the concept of leaving a little something behind to keep people from thinking you were greedy.

"Thanks, Ethan. The food was delicious."

"You're welcome." Ethan stroked his chin. "I'd like to get into the whirlpool at some point. Are you interested or do you want to rest up a while?" He looked at his wristwatch. "There's still four or five hours left until dark. If you'd like to go into San Francisco, I can always do the hot tub later."

"Are you sure about San Francisco? I don't want to spoil your plans."

He gripped her hands and looked into her eyes. "No matter where we hang out, I plan to be in your company as much as possible."

Dakota blushed. Her smile told him it was okay as she stretched her hand across the table and caressed his face.

The thrill of crossing the Golden Gate Bridge reflected in Dakota's sparkling eyes. Like so many other folks, she'd had no idea the bridge was red in color and not gold. She thought it was a massive structure, an amazingly impressive one. As the rental car rolled smoothly over the bridge, she felt both exhilaration and fear. That it was a long way down with an awful lot of water to drink had spiked her anxiety.

Much to Dakota's and Ethan's dismay, the hours had raced by. Despite the limited time, he'd gotten to whisk her to quite a few other San Francisco landmarks. She had fallen in love with Sausalito and couldn't wait to come back to Embarcadero to shop and dine in the near future. They'd also had a drink at the famous Fairmont Hotel on Nob Hill.

Still wanting to soak in the hot tub for a spell, Ethan swung the car into the parking area. He then exited the car and ran around to open the door for Dakota, who looked as if she was ready to drop. If she hadn't mentioned getting into the Jacuzzi, he wouldn't have brought it up. They'd had a wonderful time and he didn't want to ruin any part of it. They still had tomorrow, up until the early evening flight back to L.A.

"Still up for the stress-buster session in the Jacuzzi tub?" Dakota asked.

Excited by her desire to go through with the initial plan, Ethan grinned. "I was hoping you'd still want to hit the Jacuzzi. Let's get to the room and change clothes. We'll probably be too tired to do anything but laze around once we're through soaking."

"Probably so. It's getting late, anyway, and we've got an early wakeup call."

Dakota's removal of the provocative, lacy coverup revealed an alluring, basic black, one-piece swimsuit she'd had for a couple of years. The swimwear hugged her fabulous figure, with an eye-popping plunging neckline. After testing the temperature with her toes, she carefully eased her body down into the Jacuzzi tub.

The steaming water swirling about Dakota allowed her muscles to instantly react to the soothing heat. As her body relaxed further, her eyes began to droop slightly. The strong, pulsating jets massaged her legs and calves vigorously. It felt so good to just lie back and chill out for a while. Lie back and heat up, she mentally corrected.

A quick glance in Ethan's direction made Dakota smile softly. The gray and black trunks he wore were sexy, showing off rippling muscles and solid thighs. She thought his sculpted abs were a sight for sore eyes. He was the quintessential man.

Ethan was beside Dakota before she could further ponder the subject of her thoughts. She was surprised by how quickly he'd changed positions. As he rested his hand on her thigh, she had a nerve-jangling reaction to his gentle touch. Looking into her eyes, his gaze warm and tender, he slowly traced his index finger down the center of her cleavage. Her body responded once again. These kinds of heady sensations streaking through her body wreaked havoc on her composure.

It wasn't hard for Dakota to concede to the fact that she wanted Ethan in the carnal sense. This man turned her on, made her libido react wildly to his every touch. She hadn't been in a situation like this in a long time and none that ever felt this good.

Dakota moved even closer to Ethan, until their thighs touched. Reaching down into the water, she took his hand, squeezing it tightly. Feeling more than the heat from the Jacuzzi, Ethan tipped her chin with two fingers and kissed her passionately. His tongue connected with hers and the kiss grew intense. Turning in more toward him, she cupped his face in both her hands and kissed him back deeply.

In one swift movement, Ethan had Dakota straddling him. As her bottom connected with his hardened flesh, he moaned with desire. His manhood was ramrod straight and he knew she had to feel his erection right through her swimwear.

Ethan's hardness excited her beyond measure. Growing bold in her explorations, Dakota's tongue seduced his ears and throat. As she lowered her head level with his chest, she closed her eyes and tasted his erect nipples, nipping at them gently. Tasting his flesh had her wanting more. Her hands began touching his body tenderly, caressing his thighs gently, sparking hell's fire beneath his skin.

Ethan's mind was incapable of considering caution. The woman squirming around on his lap had taken the intimacy between them to another level. He was ecstatic at her taking the lead and commanding control of the tempo.

As she lifted his hands and placed them on her breasts, he'd never felt the insane sensations now gripping his loins. Although mindful of their being in a public place, he wasn't about to rein in her passion. She also knew where they were.

Dakota was free right now, freer than she'd been at the pizzeria. Sharing in her freedom had him feeling like he was on top of the universe. Ethan had to wonder if her free-flying spirit would continue once they were back behind closed doors.

In Dakota's opinion Ethan was a completely different kind of man from the one she'd dealt with. This was a guy who seemingly played by an admirable set of ethical rules. He was someone she wanted to trust explicitly. Stepping out on faith was one favorable option, unless she wanted to continue to relive the past. Staying mired in what had occurred a long time ago was a losing turn for her to take. In fact, she'd resided there for too long as it was.

Dakota didn't view herself as a loser. She was a winner who desperately wanted to believe she was capable of winning Ethan's heart. She didn't want just a physical relationship. This was about the spiritual, about the stuff that made the world go round.

CHAPTER 7

As Dakota dressed for bed, right down the hall from where Ethan was to sleep, she entertained the idea of lying with him, his arms wrapped around her tenderly. As she envisioned them together naked, a flash of heat stole through her flesh. The vividly delicious visions had her fanning off with a newspaper.

Turning off her scorching thoughts, she looked in the full-length mirror and slipped the pink silk chemise over her head. The butterflies on the gown had been hand-painted onto the creamy silk in a variety of pastel colors. Picking up the matching robe, she put it on but left the belt to hang loose. She didn't want to completely conceal the gown. The silky set was beautiful and sexy but wasn't too provocative to wear in front of Ethan. They had decided to have hot drinks together before retiring for the night.

■ ■ ■ ■

Smiling broadly, Ethan set out the cupcakes he'd purchased earlier. When Dakota had mentioned her love for carrot cake, he recalled the Oakland bakery that sold cupcakes in the same flavoring, heavily iced with a delicious cream cheese concoction.

On the way back to the hotel he'd made a short detour in hopes of putting a dazzling smile on her pretty face. The red candy apple he had given her on an earlier date had gone over big. Dakota had thanked him over and over again for his thoughtfulness.

With the bakery right next door to the bookstore they'd browsed through, Ethan had slipped out without her knowledge. The box had been stored in the trunk, so she hadn't seen it until they'd arrived back at the hotel.

Dakota walked into the cozy living area just as Ethan lowered himself down onto the sofa. As he looked up, his breath caught. "You are gorgeous. Your lingerie is beautiful. Silky, frilly and soft looks good on you."

Trying hard not to blush, Dakota failed. She smiled gently, seating herself right next to him on the sofa. "Thanks. You took in quite a lot with just one glance. I'm impressed. Men don't normally pay close attention to what women wear."

"I've heard detailed comments men make about *how* a woman is dressed. Believe me, we do pay *close* attention. I see you like butterflies."

Dakota looked down at her gown. "Butterflies are my favorite creatures. I also own a butterfly pendant and earrings fashioned out of gold, bronze and silver, a gift from my grandparents. Butterflies fly free, Ethan. I'm sure you've heard that expression before."

"I have. And you're the most beautiful butterfly. Seeing you float about is like watching a sonnet in motion." He bent his head and kissed her softly on the mouth. One kiss wasn't nearly enough, so he kissed her several more times. He then pointed over at the table. "I hear that some beautiful butterflies love carrot cake." Dakota laughed.

The cupcakes had Dakota squealing with pleasure. Rushing across the room, she picked up one and licked the swirled icing. Closing her eyes, she savored the cream cheese topping. She turned to face Ethan, holding up the treat. "You keep surprising me by how much attention you *do* pay. When exactly did you buy them?"

"Let me keep my secrets. Don't want you to figure me out too soon. I remembered that you love carrot cake. Because you showed bravery for someone who's only flown once, I thought you deserved a little treat."

Dakota blew him a kiss. "Thanks for listening to me."

"I pride myself on being a good listener." Ethan had liked Dakota's analogy. "When I don't hear what's been said, it causes me a bit of difficulty. My father asked me to call and reschedule an appointment with one of his clients. I wasn't listening to him because my mind was on something else. Dad nearly lost a client because of that. It was the last time I failed to listen."

Touched by his story, Dakota ran over to him and gave him an impassioned kiss. "Why do you insist on giving me reasons to like you? You'd better be careful. If you continue acting this way, you might just get yourself rewarded."

"Rewarded how?"

Her eyes gleamed cunningly sweet. "You'll just have to wait and see. I want it to be a big surprise, like my delicious cupcakes. Are we ready for the tea now?"

Dakota's smile and flirtatious body language had Ethan physically riled up. He knew exactly what kind of reward he'd love to have. Stripping her free of all the silky frills and butterflies hiding her naked body from view was a nice start.

Once Ethan poured two cups of chai, he carefully handed one to Dakota. Moving as close to her on the sofa as he could get, he grinned. "Here's to my reward." He raised his cup to toast. "I can hardly wait to get it."

And I can't wait to give it to you. Dakota smiled at her thoughts. The couple sat quietly, sipping tea, munching on cupcakes.

The urge to kiss Ethan revisited Dakota. Instead of giving any consideration to it, she tenderly coiled her arms around his neck. As her mouth set his aflame, audible moans escaped him. As she continued to shower his mouth with blistering kisses, her fingers twisted in his hair. She could feel both their hearts hammering away.

Ethan kissed her back, his tongue plunging in and out of her mouth. Her hands ran up and down his back, making him desperate with wanting. Despite knowing this sweet encounter would soon end, she never wanted it to. Delightful sensations trickled all through her inner core, but she wasn't ready to surrender her all to him just yet.

That didn't mean they couldn't play a

little longer.

Dipping a finger in the icing, laughing, she smeared it on Ethan's lips and ate it off. Her playful mood was encouraging and had him scooping up icing and dabbing it on her nose, cheeks, throat and lips. His tongue enjoyed a deliciously sweet journey, the tip of it flicking away the delectable creamy frosting.

Tossing her head back, exposing her throat, she shivered with ecstasy as his tongue traveled all the way down to her cleavage. Their eyes met and locked as he lowered the robe down around her shoulders, revealing the spaghetti straps on her gown. His lips tracing her bare skin with soft kisses was erotic for both him and Dakota.

Ethan blazed a trail of heat all over the exposed parts of her flesh. The feel of her firm breasts filling his hands caused him to tremble within. A dab of frosting onto each of her nipples made her breathing quicken. Holding his head in place made it all worthwhile for him. His hands traveled lower and lower. Pushing up the hemline of her gown, he dipped his head and covered her thighs with moist kisses, inching closer and closer to the core of her femininity. Her soft moans were sweet music to his ears, but he knew when to cool things off. In his heart he knew Dakota wasn't ready for the ultimate experience.

Dakota knew exactly why Ethan had pulled back despite how much they'd both enjoyed their romantic rendezvous. She was glad he was tuned into her emotions. Her feelings for him were strengthening by the moment.

Getting to her feet slowly, Dakota wasn't ready to call it a night, but she was tired. She enjoyed the time spent with Ethan. It had given her more important information about him. She had earlier enjoyed hearing how he'd grown up and the principles of honor instilled in him. This wise man spoke his mind, without filtering his thoughts, yet he still imparted information carefully. He was real.

Ethan slid his arm around Dakota's shoulder, squeezing gently. "I'll walk you to your bedroom. I can see how tired you are. I'll try not to be too noisy while I clean up around here. Don't want housekeeping thinking pigs occupied this room."

His sense of humor intrigued her, making her laugh. "I can hang in a little longer. I don't mind helping you put everything back in order."

He shook his head. "Got it covered. Rinsing out the cups, washing the utensils and wiping off the counter and table will be the extent of it. Like you, I'm bushed. Come on, let me help you settle in."

Her hand went up to his face, stroking it with gentleness. "This has been an amazing experience. Thanks to you, I feel really good." She laughed softly, holding dear to her heart the countless, never-to-be-forgotten memories. She believed there was more unforgettable times to come.

Ethan pulled back the duvet cover and the top sheet. She sat down on the bed and he removed her slippers. His arm went around her shoulder and his hand slid under the back of her knees to support her legs. Aligning himself just right, he lifted her, laid her on the mattress and covered her up. He looked down into Dakota's eyes. "Thanks for coming to Oakland with me. I've had fun. Hope tomorrow is more of the same."

"The fun has been nonstop. No doubt it will continue." She reached for Ethan and brought his head down level with hers. She kissed him passionately, thoroughly. "See you in the morning."

"I'm looking forward to sharing a sunrise with you. Good night."

"Let's make it a point to watch the sun come up together," she requested.

Nothing could've pleased him more. "Let's set the alarms. See you a couple of minutes before sunrise." He leaned down and kissed her with the same deep passion they'd shared all evening. Dakota's heart filled with sentiment. Tomorrow, she thought. They'd come a long way from where it had all begun.

Using his fingertips, he closed her eyelids. "Go to sleep." He quickly got to his feet and then reached down and turned off the bedside lamp. Without uttering another word, yet wanting like crazy to slip into bed with her, he left the room, quietly closing the door behind him. Ethan stood there for a moment, wondering about their tomorrows.

Feeling exhilarated over all that had transpired, Dakota laid her head back on the pillow. She'd taken numerous unprecedented risks with Ethan. So far, they had all paid off. The losses she'd had were great, but the recently experienced gains had taken on amazing momentum.

Standing behind Dakota, arms wrapped around her waist, his chin resting atop her head, Ethan looked up at the morning's masterpiece slowly rising on the horizon.

"Amazing," Dakota commented, nearly

breathless at the sight before her. "This sunrise is spectacular. Look at the colors bursting loose all around it, a mixture of soft orange, fiery reds and bright yellow. The blue skies and white clouds are a fabulous backdrop. The sun hangs imperiously, providing light for the entire universe. Awesome!"

Ethan brushed back her windblown hair. "I know what you mean. So are you."

"That makes two of us. Thanks for taking such good care of me."

Ethan leaned down and kissed the top of her head. "It's been a pleasure."

"It was nice waking up knowing we'd share a beautiful sunrise."

Ethan didn't respond. The frog in his throat was a huge one. This woman was driving him wild and he wasn't sure it was her intent. Intentional or not, it was happening. To celebrate the sunrise Ethan and Dakota kissed fervently.

Amazed at the size of the football field, not to mention the number of fans already seated inside the humongous stadium, Dakota's eyes darted everywhere, trying to take in all areas of the Oakland-Alameda County Coliseum, home of the once highly revered Oakland Raiders.

Dakota had never seen any professional sports game live and this was one exciting event. Faces painted silver and black was hilarious to her, but it also showed how committed these Raider fans were to their struggling home team.

As the national anthem began to play, Dakota and Ethan stood, placing their hands over their hearts. The patriotic anthem often brought her to tears. She loved this great country as much as anyone.

Once everyone was reseated, Dakota felt the electrifying excitement all around her. As the opening kickoff took place, the Raider fans began to rev up. Ethan was out of his seat, shouting and cheering loudly for his favorite team. The six-time Super Bowl champions, the Pittsburgh Steelers, were the guest team. An enormous number of fans wore Raiders gear, but there were a lot of opposing fans in the crowd.

These animated folks who dared to wear black and gold were no less enthusiastic about the game than the home team fans were. In fact, there were a few fearless Steelers fans loudly making no bones about their team being the best in the NFL. At the moment, the heckling between the two factions was pretty tame, but Ethan knew the demeanors could change drastically, without a moment's notice. For Dakota's sake, Ethan hoped the fans didn't turn too rowdy.

Ethan watched with amusement as his date got really deep into the game, cheering just as loud as anyone else. What was hilarious was her rooting for both teams. Whatever team scored, she clapped with enthusiasm, yelling loudly. She looked content and he was pleased by it. The exhilarating look in her eyes caused his heart to catch fire. The burning heat from the flames was all-consuming.

Dakota suddenly turned and threw her arms around Ethan's neck, hugging him tight. "Thanks so much for bringing me to Oakland with you," she shouted near his ear. "The entire trip has been awesome." Looking into his eyes, she kissed him tenderly on the mouth.

Surprise after surprise from Dakota kept catching Ethan off guard, which was rare. "I was happy you agreed to come with me. I wanted this trip to be special for you."

"It is special, Ethan. It really is."

Ethan kissed her again, his body feeling feverish all over. Giving little thought to the number of people around them, he kissed her passionately, just the way he'd desired to kiss her since day one.

This trip kept getting better and better,

Ethan thought. He didn't know where things would stand between them by the return flight home, but he felt optimistic. Dakota no longer looked like a frightened doe caught in the headlights of an oncoming car. That was a big plus. He hoped she had begun to trust him simply because he was trustworthy.

But then there was Dan.

Dakota and Ethan ran fast through the airport terminal to try to catch their flight. Whenever they lost track of everything but each other, Ethan knew it meant they'd both had a great time. He'd used poor judgment in doing more sightseeing after the Raiders' loss. Time hadn't gotten away as much as traffic jams had made them late.

As the plane backed away from the Jetway, Ethan looked at Dakota and hunched his shoulders. He hoped she wouldn't blame him for missing the plane. She had mentioned wanting to get back to L.A. before it got too late. His promise to make it happen had failed.

Getting assigned to the next flight hadn't taken Ethan very long. There were plenty of seats left to accommodate standby passengers. This particular airline was smart enough to make flying experiences a lot easier for their patrons.

Dakota felt more relaxed than she did when this journey had first begun, but she had grown apprehensive in the past few minutes. Getting back home to check on her sister was all she could think of. *Just check on her by phone,* the little voice inside her head instructed. It made perfect sense. She couldn't believe how uptight she'd gotten over something that could be handled with ease.

Dakota stepped over to Ethan. "Please excuse me for a few minutes." She kissed him on the cheek and then hurried off.

Assuming Dakota was heading for the ladies' room, Ethan watched after her. As she stopped just short of the bathroom entrance, he saw her flip open her cell phone. The mystery man in her life immediately came to his mind.

Was she calling Dan? Was he the reason she wanted to get back to L.A. before it got too late?

Ethan was once again puzzled by the relationship between Dakota and this man she called Dan, confused by his significance in her life. But he was far more perplexed by her actions. Why had she flown to Oakland with him if she had another man in her life, a guy she obviously cared enough about to keep in close contact with? Perhaps this was the same man who'd broken her heart, a guy she couldn't seem to shake. Stranger things than staying involved with an ex-lover had happened, even one who'd hurt you.

Ethan couldn't omit the fact that she had never agreed to an exclusive relationship the second time he'd brought it up. Nor was he sure it was actually Dan she was phoning.

With Dakota on her way back to where he was now seated, Ethan dismissed all thoughts of this mystery man she'd spoken of on several occasions. If he wasn't bold enough to step up to the plate and ask her about it, he needed to let it go until he was.

One thing was for sure, Dan was in between her and him. He wanted the man gone, but it really wasn't up to him. It was about what Dakota wanted. Ethan silently made a vow to himself. If she brought up Dan one more time, he was asking all the questions that had been building up in his mind. If she didn't bring him up, he'd have to play it by ear.

Dakota sat down next to Ethan and looped her arm through his. Feeling bone-tired, she laid her head on his shoulder. Danielle was fine, according to the head nurse. After playing cards with a staff member, she'd played with her dolls and had also watched some Nickelodeon. Danielle was expected to fall asleep any minute. Dakota was disappointed that she wouldn't see her sister this evening. With God willing, they'd have a wealth of tomorrows.

Persia picked up the phone at Licensed to Thrill. She hoped this call was the last one of the evening. She was ready to go home, but her duties had to be handled. She greeted the caller with an enthusiasm she didn't quite feel.

Luke smiled as Persia's teasing voice whispered to him in a sexy tone. "This is Luke Lockhart. Surprised to hear from me again?"

"I'm rarely surprised by anything. Are you in the bedroom?" She decided to set the tempo for this conversation. No more personal stuff.

"I'm stretched out in the bathtub, bubbles up to my neck."

"I know what I'd do if I were bathing with you."

"I want to know. Tell me."

"I'd lather you up in more ways than one. Tubs are small, so I'd have to straddle you for comfort." She moaned softly. "Are you feeling me?"

"Right down to my sex, where I burn hot for you."

"How hot are you? How hot do you want to get?"

"Desert hot, baby, dry and prickly."

"I love the way your body feels beneath my hands. Love the hard abs and the hard . . ." She laughed throatily. "How do my hands feel all over your body?"

"Finish what you were going to say. Make me sweat."

"From every pore. Hmm, I love your hardware. Is it ready for me?"

"Readier than it has ever been. Ooh, that feels so good. I love the way you wiggle that sweet behind of yours. Do that again."

"Give it to me, sweetie, every hard inch. I'm wet from more than just the water."

Glad it was Friday, the last day of work this week, Dakota stripped out of her black dress slacks and white silk blouse and hung them in the closet. A quick shower was first on her agenda. She had a couple of hours before Ethan was expected to drop in. He had called earlier to ask if she was free, offering to bring over a couple of movies to watch. She had been enthusiastically up for his suggestion. He had also mentioned bringing along dinner, asking her what her taste buds were in the mood for. She'd told him to feel free to choose. They both knew the kinds of food each favored.

Dakota had hit the shower running. As the cold water pelted down her body, she came alive. For the past couple of nights she had stayed up late studying because a test was scheduled for the following week. She was getting closer and closer to graduation. Sometimes it was hard to believe she'd soon have her degree. If all went as planned, she'd graduate in less than a year. Getting her teaching credentials would be one of the happiest days of her life.

Dakota rapidly dried off with a fluffy towel and then applied creamy lotion all over her body. She took special care of her feet. She brushed her long hair into a ponytail and wrapped a decorative band around it. After pulling on a pair of crisply creased blue jeans and donning a simple white T-shirt, she rather looked like the all-American girl from next door.

Grabbing her English textbook from off the shelf, Dakota stretched out on the bed. As she paid special attention to the material she expected to be covered on the test, she became engrossed in her studies.

English was Dakota's favorite subject, but special education was where her heart was. She wanted desperately to teach young children with the same sort of issues Danielle experienced. These kids were so special, so warm and loving. She smiled as she thought about all the hugs and kisses her little sister had given her the day after she'd returned home from Oakland. Danielle hadn't a single clue that Dakota had been out of town.

Finished going over her English materials, Dakota picked up a book about special education, hoping to get more of a feel for the job she'd soon take on. There was lots of great information in the glossary. She'd long ago lost track of the number of publications she'd perused about special education and Down syndrome. Dakota was well-informed on the subject matter.

Down syndrome was a set of mental and physical symptoms that resulted from having an extra copy of chromosome 21. Even though people with this health challenge may have some physical and mental features in common, symptoms can range from mild to severe. Despite being incurable, early intervention helped some people live productive lives well into adulthood. Children diagnosed with this malady can often benefit from speech therapy, occupational therapy and exercise for gross and fine motor skills. Many children can integrate into regular classes at school.

Danielle fell into the mild classification, yet she still required special attention. Her motor skills were fine and she had benefited greatly from speech therapy at an early age. Her communication skills were remarkable.

That she'd lost track of time didn't surprise Dakota when the doorbell rang. She often got lost in her studies. In her opinion, she could never be over-informed.

Dashing into the bathroom, she picked up the brush and gave her hair a few brisk strokes. Using a bushy cosmetic brush, she dusted her face with a matte finish. A quick dab of clear lip gloss came next. Satisfied with her appearance, she rushed to the front of her apartment. Although Dakota was sure it was Ethan on the other side of the door, she looked through the security peephole, anyway. Her eyes lit up, sparkling like diamonds.

CHAPTER 8

Dakota and Ethan greeted each other with a passionate kiss. The ice had been shattered in Oakland. The weeks since then in each other's company had actually warmed things up.

"Come on in. Here, let me take a couple of these bags. Looks like you bought out the place. I don't know what it is, but my nose is shouting Italian."

Ethan grinned. "Right on the money. Perhaps the Olive Garden logo on the bags helped out," he teased.

Dakota giggled. "I'm caught."

As Dakota led the way into the kitchen, Ethan followed along behind her. Although he was still worried about what secrets she held in her heart, he still wanted that exclusive relationship. *How deep could her secrets be? If she had so much to hide, why would she continue to share her time and home with him?*

Dakota's mouth watered as she removed several aluminum containers from the large shopping bag. Rushing over to the cabinet, she pulled out several bowls to serve the food. As she dumped the angel hair pasta into one casserole, the scent of marinara was heavenly. Another container was chock-full of big, beefy meatballs submerged in zesty tomato sauce. Next was fettuccine.

Ethan held up a bread stick. "Have you had these before?"

"You better believe it. I can't wait to sink my teeth into the soft dough. I don't eat bread too often, but the sticks from Olive Garden are a special treat for me."

Ethan and Dakota set the table and then put out the food.

The couple sat down to eat a short time later and he passed a humble blessing.

Dakota rolled back her eyes dramatically. "This marinara is so good. I'd love to have their recipe."

"You won't get any argument here. But pasta always seems to taste better the next day, once the sauce saturates. I won't take anything away from what it tastes like right now. I'm pleased."

"The fettuccine is good, too. My grandmother knew how to fix pasta like this. Then again, there weren't too many foods she

184

didn't have you begging for more. Mom was a good cook, but she was no match for Grandma."

Ethan chuckled. "We might need to jog around the block a few times after this meal. Either that or fall right off to sleep. Up for some exercise?"

"Depends on what you brought along for dessert."

"Chocolate éclairs."

Dakota moaned. "Why couldn't you have said fresh fruit?"

" 'Cause that's not what I picked up from the bakery."

They both cracked up.

"Bring on the éclairs," he enthused, kissing the tips of his fingers.

Leaving the dishes to tackle later, Dakota and Ethan strolled hand-in-hand into the living room and dropped down on the sofa. He picked up from the coffee table the movies he'd brought along. "Hope you haven't seen any of these."

Dakota glanced at the DVD cases. "I've seen this one a dozen times or more," she said, pointing at *Hitch,* another of Danielle's favorite movies starring Will Smith. "Wish I could get to the theaters more, but it's not always possible."

"We'll just have to try to remedy that," he said. "I recall a time when I went to the theater every weekend. I still go a lot, but not nearly as much as before. Watching films at home is more relaxing for me."

"Me, too." She thought of all the DVDs she and Danielle watched. They'd probably frequent movie theaters if the circumstances were different.

"I normally purchase my DVD movies when they're first released. After work on Tuesdays, the weekday when the new ones came out, I can be found standing in line."

"I do that a lot myself." Looking into Dakota's eyes, Ethan leaned forward and feathered several kisses onto her lower lip. In a loving gesture, he gently combed through her hair with his fingers. "You look good and taste so sweet." Unable to hold back, he took fiery possession of her mouth.

For Dakota, it felt good to have a man hold her this close and kiss her so tenderly. Ethan seemed to care a lot about her, patient in allowing her to grow more and more comfortable with him. Clasping her hands together behind his head, she kissed him back with fervor.

The phone suddenly rang, startling them both. Rapidly, they pulled apart. Appearing slightly embarrassed, Dakota reached for the receiver. "Yes, it's Dakota. What's going on?" As she listened to the caller's message, her eyes widened. "Danni? What's wrong with Danni? Please tell me what's happening."

Ethan got up from the sofa, hastily distancing himself from Dakota. It seemed old Danny boy was back again. Ethan now realized he'd never left. The man was right in between them — on a regular basis. *How was he to combat someone unknown to him?* No matter how he felt about the situation or the name she continued to call, he didn't like seeing her so upset about whatever news she'd received.

"I'll be right there. Thanks for calling." Dakota hung up the phone and leaped off the sofa. "Sorry, but I've got to go out. I have an emergency to deal with."

Her curt, easy dismissal of him stung Ethan hard. His eyes narrowed briefly. "You seem pretty upset. Maybe I should drive you where you need to go."

Dakota shook her head. "No, that's not necessary, but thanks for the offer." Danielle was having difficulty breathing; the doctor was treating her now. Without uttering another word, she ran toward the bedroom. After snatching up her purse, she closed her eyes and began praying fervently for Danielle. "God, please, let her be okay. Please."

Dakota felt guilty for how she treated Ethan, but she didn't know how to handle this situation any other way. Keeping Danielle a secret from him was wrong. He'd probably be furious with her when she finally told him the truth. She would tell him, she promised herself. It was just a matter of how, when and where.

Danielle was a strong, independent little girl, but she was still vulnerable in some ways. She was so young when their parents and grandparents died, but she wasn't too young to not remember the family they once had. Dakota's heart fluttered when she thought of their time of grief.

Another loss could occur for Danielle if she got to know Ethan and then one day he just upped and left. She now trusted Ethan with her heart, but she worried about involving Danielle in something that wasn't a guarantee. Was it fair for her to compromise her sister's heart, too?

Standing at the front door of her apartment, Dakota slowly turned to face Ethan, trying desperately to choose the right words to say. "Sorry our evening has to end so abruptly. I have no choice. Okay if I call you later, when I get back home?"

Hardly able to believe his ears, Ethan grimaced.

Why would she want to call him later when he was there with her right now? Hadn't he offered to take her wherever she had to go? Running off to this Dan person was obviously more important to her than sharing the evening with him. The phone conversation sounded like the guy was in some kind of trouble. Maybe it *was* a real emergency.

Three was a crowd in this relationship. Now would be an acceptable time frame for Dan the man to do a total disappearing act, Ethan fumed.

The anger slowly bubbling to the surface inside Ethan matched the scowl on his face. Dakota would have to choose. He didn't plan to hang around much longer without a commitment from her. He turned on his heels and stormed off.

Stunned and shaken by the way Ethan had departed, Dakota ran outside, staring after him. Sorry she'd hurt him, she put her hand over her heart. "Ethan, I plan to make it up to you," she whispered. "If coming clean about Danielle is what I need to do, so be it. I don't want you to disappear from my life." Tears fell from her eyes as she watched Ethan get into his car and speed off.

Dakota wondered if Ethan had room in

his heart for a sweet little girl whose only desire was to be loved. An exclusive love affair was possible for her and Ethan, but if it came down to a permanent situation, it had to be a package deal.

As Dakota recalled how Ethan had rushed off, it occurred to her that he might think she was seeing another man. She had said Danni in front of Ethan on a few occasions. Making a silent promise to call him, after she was briefed on her sister's health, she ran to her car and turned off the alarm. Once inside her automobile, she wasted no time.

Ethan had followed her for the sole purpose of discovery. Following a woman's movements wasn't something he'd ever done before; he didn't like the way it made him feel. He wasn't a stalker, yet his actions were disproving.

Parking his car outside the huge lot, he waited for Dakota to appear. His wait was short-lived. He watched in silence as she moved at a fast pace, practically running. Because there were several structures in the vicinity, he wasn't sure which one she'd enter. It was dark outside, but the large overhead lights allowed him to make out the name on the tall gray building she'd just disappeared into.

"Center of the Courageous Heart," he read aloud the name. Wondering what type of place it was, he looked at the inscription below the name. It appeared to be a medical facility.

Ethan's mind began to scatter. Who was Dan and why was he at this medical facility, if in fact it was him who was inside? The answers to his questions had to come from Dakota. Was he willing to let her know he'd followed her to try to find out what and who was coming between them? What would she think of the methods he'd used to track her?

Pacing the floor outside the private room, Dakota was beside herself with anxiety. Doctors and nurses hovered around Danielle, working on her tiny body. All Dakota had learned was that her sister had breathing problems. This was a new medical dilemma. No breathing disorders were in her medical history.

Dr. Pete Simpson came outside the room and rushed over to the window where Dakota stood looking out at the star-studded sky above. He extended his hand to her, smiling sympathetically. "I'm not sure what's happening with Danielle, but Dr. Alexander is on the way." Stephanie

Alexander was Danielle's lifelong pediatrician.

Dakota smiled weakly. "Thank you, Dr. Simpson. How's Danni doing?"

"She's having a rough time of it. A nurse just happened to be in the room when she began struggling for air. If it was asthma, we probably would've had it under control by now. So far she's not responding to treatment. She's hooked up to a breathing apparatus. We'll know more after Dr. Alexander does her preliminary exams. I've already ordered blood gas studies to check her oxygen levels."

"Is her life being threatened?" Dakota nervously ran her palms up and down the sides of her face.

Dr. Simpson shook his head. "No one can make that kind of call in the absence of a specific diagnosis. We have to wait and see what the test results indicate."

"You're right, of course." As though she were lost in a daze, Dakota walked over to the window where she could look in on what was happening with Danielle. The little girl's eyes were closed. It looked as if she were asleep. There were no signs of her struggling to breathe. That was definitely a positive, Dakota concluded.

A couple of hours passed since Dakota

had first arrived at the facility. She had tried her best to stay calm and patient, but she was running critically low in both areas. Seeing Dr. Alexander coming toward her, she sighed with relief and got to her feet.

The two well-acquainted females embraced.

"Let's sit down," Dr. Alexander suggested to Dakota.

Out of respect for the physician, Dakota waited until Dr. Alexander was seated before she sat back down.

"I know you're probably out of your mind with worry, so let me give it to you straight. Danielle had an allergic reaction to seafood. It's all under control and she's fine. However, she can never eat seafood again. Iodine is at issue here. It's off-limits, including iodine contrasts used in some forms of radiology testing."

"Thank you so much." Dakota wiped away the tears of relief. "Why weren't they able to diagnosis this in the beginning? Aren't seafood allergies common?"

"I understand your concerns, but I don't want to second-guess my colleagues. However, the absence of hives is my best guess. Hives almost always accompany this type of allergy. They just didn't show up right away. As soon as the red swellings began to pop out, Danielle was treated with a Benadryl shot . . . and she responded immediately."

Dakota nodded. "Thank God. What about iodine wash?"

"Some people are allergic to iodine and not to the wash. However, I simply wouldn't risk it. In the form of big red stickers, iodine allergy alerts will be placed on her medical records and facility charts. Any time you take her to see a doctor, dentist or other health-care provider, they need to know about the allergy. Do you have any other questions for me?"

"Is she breathing okay or does she still need the machine?"

"Danielle is able to breathe just fine on her own. The machine will be used as a precautionary measure until after the IV treatments are completed."

Dr. Alexander went on to let Dakota know exactly how allergies to seafood and iodine affected a person's ability to breathe, mentioning swelling of the throat.

On her way home Dakota pulled over to the side of the road to collect her jittery nerves. Resting her forehead against the steering wheel, she considered putting in a call to Ethan. Maybe she could drop by to see him. Perhaps they could make up, but she'd have some explaining to do. By the fifth ring, he hadn't answered. Disappointment trickled through her. She had hoped for a different outcome. She wanted to see Ethan and needed to find comfort in the strength of his powerful arms.

Dakota knew another lonely night was ahead of her as she let herself into the apartment. She had forgotten to turn on the bedside lamp, so there was no light to guide her way. Carefully she made her way into the bedroom, stripping out of her clothes as she went along. She hung up the garments and then made her way into the bathroom.

Inside the shower Dakota released more tears. But relief wasn't just a crying jag away. Not in this instance.

Bone-weary, she stepped out of the shower. Seated on the dressing-table stool, she dried off her body from top to bottom, rubbing so hard she barely noticed the trembling of her hands. *Ethan, where are you? What are you thinking? I need you so much.*

Fighting back her emotions, she sprinkled her body with scented powder and rubbed it into her flesh. This was one night she wanted to fall right off to sleep, but she felt it might be hard to achieve. There was just so much scary stuff on her mind.

Dakota wandered into the bedroom and over to the dresser, pulling from the middle drawer a pair of black silk pajamas. After slipping into a robe, she went out to the kitchen to warm up some of the Italian leftovers, wishing Ethan was there to share them. It was hard for her to concede this relationship. It wasn't over; not if she had her way.

Less angry than he had been earlier in the week, Ethan had found an escape by spending more time working on his book. He'd lost count of how often he'd considered calling Dakota to see if they could work things out, but he'd changed his mind every single time. He needed to let her come to him if he didn't want to give the impression he was running after her. Ethan wasn't into chasing women.

Would he fight for their relationship?

If Dakota gave him hope. If she showed he had something to fight for. Yes, Ethan concluded, he'd fight with every fiber of his being. Placing his pad and pen within easy reach on his desk, he picked up the phone and hit Redial.

This shift was a long, boring one for Persia. She had received only three calls. On each one she'd had to be extremely creative. Each of the patrons had wanted melting hot, sexy conversation. She'd succeeded in giving them their money's worth, but the calls had ended quicker than most, which hurt the paycheck.

Dakota looked over at the phone dial. The flashing white blinker signaled a call waiting. Maybe she would end up earning her average for the shift after all. If a few more clients were kept on the phone long enough, perhaps it'd all turn out worthwhile. She picked up the receiver and clicked on the caller.

"Hey, there, Ms. Persia."

Persia smiled broadly. This guy with the now-familiar voice was starting to grow on her. "I thought about you recently. Didn't think I'd hear from you, though."

"Are you kidding? Your honesty and openness scores a lot of points. I like you."

Persia laughed. "Either you're tired of the porn industry or just plain bored."

"I called because I needed to talk to someone. I'm dealing with some serious issues and needed a break from all the drama."

"Let me get this right. You're paying all this money just to talk to someone about your issues? Don't you have a best friend to help you out? What about a therapist?"

"The money I'm spending is well worth it. Your voice has a calming effect on me. Plus, you're a perfect stranger and I don't have to worry about you telling anyone about my problems. Friends can be judgmental. I'm making no sense at all, am I?"

Persia ran her fingers through her hair. "You're making perfect sense. And your secrets are safe. I promise."

"In that case, why don't we get together and have coffee. Then I can tell you about all the stuff I'm trying to handle, unsuccessfully, I might add."

"Sorry, but I can't do that. We have to stick with the phone calls."

"So you can get paid, right?"

Luke's remark made Persia feel awful. "This *is* my job. And you knew that from the first time you called in."

"If we become really good friends, think I can call you at a number that won't cost me an arm and a leg?"

"Don't do this to me. You're my client and that's as far as it can go."

"Well, I guess I'll just spend a couple of hundred dollars more by telling you what's happening in my life. I'm in love with a girl who I don't think is in love with me. I'd be embarrassed to tell this to my close friends."

"What makes you think she doesn't love you, Luke?"

"It's not so obvious. I just have a hunch. We know when love is absent, but we can go into denial. How do you think I can win this girl's heart?"

"Simply being yourself. I must admit I wasn't too keen on you in the beginning. Does the lady know what your job is?"

"Noooo," he drawled. "She probably wouldn't go out with me again if she did. I'm deceiving her, aren't I?"

Persia sucked in a deep breath. "Major deceit . . . and there's no kinder word for it." Persia knew that for a fact. She was a pro at it.

"You're right, but I hate admitting it. Mind if I call you again? I need help through this crisis."

"It'll be costly. Maybe in time I'll share with you a few of my issues. I never dreamed we'd become confidants," Persia joked.

"Go figure!" He cleared his throat. "I'll have to charge you when you confide in me. That's only fair, don't you think?"

"You got me there. I'll just be your confidante and keep my problems to myself."

"El cheapo, huh! With all the money you make, you're not willing to share it."

"Not a single penny. By the way, if you're

so in love, how do you justify having sex with all those other women? Don't you fear contracting communicable diseases and infecting her?"

"Condoms are a requirement. Testing for diseases occurs more than you could ever imagine. The company I work for is first-rate. They make sure their staff is healthy. I don't try to justify it because it can't be. And we haven't made love yet."

Persia was trying not to form a negative opinion of Luke. She wasn't a hypocritical person, but here she was criticizing his career choice. She was no different from him, no better than he. She may not have actual sex for money, but she vocally simulated the act to earn a paycheck. She wasn't in any position to judge. "Sorry about the rude questions. Hope I didn't offend you."

"It's impossible to offend someone in my line of work. We have thick skin and no scruples." He laughed. "I have sex for a living. And I'm good at it. Everyone needs a day off from what they do best. I'm taking today."

Luke wondered what kind of person Persia really was. If nothing else, she was certainly interesting. She had a sweet quality about her and he liked how she came right out with whatever she wanted to say.

Not everyone spoke their mind so effort-lessly.

"Besides your job in adult films, do you have hobbies?" She sensed that he wasn't all that interested in a sexual conversation.

"Several. Tennis and hiking are high on my list. Reading is at the top. I read a variety of genres, but I love stories written by Walter Moseley. I'm actually writing a book myself."

"About the work you do?"

"Pretty much. I haven't pinned down one particular topic to expound upon. The sex industry has so many facets I can write about. Do you like to read?"

"Romance. What do you think of that?"

"Romance is good, but so many perfect endings are a big stretch."

"That's what many women love. Romance is an escape into fairy-tale land for some of us. It's fiction, but we love perfect endings. It also gives hope."

"I can see that happening. I try to stay hopeful. We're living in rough times and we need softer measures to change some of our harsher realities."

"I'm with you on that, Luke. I know you didn't call to be grilled. Sorry."

"You *are* an inquisitive one. Your questions give me a lot to chew on. Now I'd like to know why you do what you do, Persia."

"To get the bills paid."

"Is it really that simple?"

"It is to me. Seems like we're both in our jobs because of what it pays. There's no mystery in that. Most of the people I work with do this job for the same reason."

"Money can make a person do lots of things they wouldn't otherwise do."

"For me, it's the lack of money. This is the only job I've been interviewed for that allows me to earn way above minimum wage. But I plan to get out of this business real soon. There are dreams I want to fulfill."

"I know what you mean. Tell me how you came to even apply for the job."

"It was recommended to me by another employee, one of my classmates. I saw it as a means to an end. She dug herself out from under a mountain of debts by working here. It has taken some real getting used to, but I'm paying the rent."

"What'd you have to get used to?"

"Talking sexy. I wasn't too good at it in the beginning. Guilt is real."

"You may not believe this, but I was too excited to function properly on my first adult film role." He cracked up. "I can't believe I just told you that."

Persia laughed, too. "I can't believe we're

telling our employment secrets to each other. This is one weird conversation. Are you sure you're not a recruiter for your company? Sounds to me like you're gathering information for an article or something."

"I could say the same about you. You've asked a lot of questions, too."

"Looks like we're both inquisitive and we're both in the sex industry. Who am I to judge, anyway?"

"I wish more people saw it that way. I'm judged all the time. I still haven't learned how to let it completely roll off my back. Out of all the guys who call you for X-rated conversations, what types do you like best?"

Persia chuckled. "I prefer the shy ones, men who feel guilty about calling me up in the first place."

"That's real interesting. Do married men ever call you?"

"More often than the single guys."

"What about single ones who are in a committed relationship?"

"They're some of the world's worst. They're not married, so they think calling in is not cheating. They even tell me it helps them be more open with their mate."

"Imagine that. Do you think they're cheating?"

"It's not being faithful and you already

know that."

"Do any of your clients see you as a confidante?"

"Most definitely." Persia laughed softly. "What is this, twenty questions? You sure are getting more and more inquisitive by the minute."

He laughed, too. "I've always got a question on the tip of my tongue about one thing or another. I'm curious by nature. Do my questions bother you?"

"Not when you're running up a tab." She laughed in hopes of softening the comment. She hadn't meant it to be harsh, but she had told the truth. The more they talked, the more money she got paid.

"Would you talk to me if you weren't getting paid?" he asked out of curiosity.

"Probably so, because we're now on a different footing."

"We are, aren't we? As I said before, I like you."

"I like you, too. You're really cool . . . and easy to talk with."

"Remarks like those really get my juices going. I'm flattered. Thank you, Persia."

"You're welcome."

"Would you mind telling me a little bit about your family?"

"Strictly off-limits. There's no point

because you'll never meet them."

"You sure about that?"

"I'm positive. Now let's move on, okay?"

The questions about her darting through his mind were downright dizzying. Knowing Persia would never reveal anything to him about her real life, he decided not to push her for answers. However, he thought they might explain a lot of things.

Luke yawned.

"Are you sleepy?"

He shoved his hand through his hair. "I am. We'll talk soon. I want to know more about you. I need to know what drives you." He looked at his watch. "Ouch, this call is going to cost me big time. But conversing with you was worth every single penny. Good night, Persia."

As she hung up the phone, she smiled, wondering if Luke Lockart was the kind of friend she needed. This particular conversation had been more personal than the others. She'd also exceeded her time quota.

Picking up the receiver, Ethan held it in his hand for a couple of minutes before cradling it. Life had been very difficult for him over the past few days. As discouraged as he was about his relationship with Dakota, it was only her who could make his heart soar.

Nothing compared to a heart with wings. He had thought that not calling her for a while was in his best interest. That theory was no longer working for him. He suffered from deprivation. His stubborn stance had denied him of her company.

Dakota had left him several messages, asking him to call her back, but he'd ignored the desperate plea he'd heard in her voice. However, not talking to her wasn't getting him anywhere. If he let another day go by without talking to her, it might turn out to be one of the worst decisions he'd ever made.

His fingers jabbed hard at the phone buttons. Holding his breath, he prayed she'd be there to pick up the call. If not, he'd try her cell phone next. He was in this all the way. As his prayer was finally answered, he smiled, looking upward. "I haven't called in a while, but I'm calling now. I miss you, Dakota. Can we talk?"

"Of course we can. I miss you, too. I'm sorry for what happened the last time we were together. I was wrong. Please forgive me."

"We both have been wrong. What are you doing right now? I can come by."

"Just kind of piddling around here until *Grey's Anatomy* comes on."

He consulted his watch. "That's a good ways off. If it's okay for me to come over, I can get there long before then."

"I'd love to see you, Ethan."

CHAPTER 9

Ethan was grateful for the delicious club sandwiches he and Dakota had made and eaten, accompanied with sides of salads, potato chips and soft drinks. He had eaten three sandwiches to her one.

Things were a little awkward for him as he sat next to her on the sofa. It had taken them a while to become comfortable with each other again. Trying to get back to square one was harder than he'd expected. There'd been no kiss or hug upon his arrival; uncertainty had kept him from moving on his desires.

Ethan continued to discreetly move closer and closer to Dakota. After a couple of minutes had passed, he gently took hold of her hand. She squeezed his fingers, making him feel relieved.

"I was being honest when I said I missed you," said Ethan.

"I believed you. I was so lonely and hated

not being able to talk to you."

Her comments lifted him up. He smiled at her to show his appreciation. "I was lonely for you, too. To help me keep my sanity I practically poured myself into my writing project. Still, I can't tell you how many times I thought about calling you."

"I wish you *had* phoned. Not hearing from you was sheer agony. I missed you."

His fingernail traced tiny circles onto her palm, causing a tingling sensation to run through her. "Besides missing me, what have you been up to lately?"

"Work at school and at my job has made Dakota a total bore. When I wasn't working, I was lost in my thoughts of you." She looked pensive. "There is so much I'd like to tell you, but I'm not ready to go there yet. Too many issues in my life are unresolved. I don't want to hurt you, and certainly not intentionally. I'm awfully confused . . . and I've been that way a good portion of my life."

"What are you so perplexed about?"

Dakota shrugged. "Life . . . and what it takes to be successful at it, to be happy in it. I have had to deal with endless things, the expected and the unexpected. I'm responsible for a lot of stuff. I stay on top of things as much as I can. I tackle the problems the best I can."

Ethan looked closely at Dakota, as if he were really seeing her for the first time, as if he could see through to the very core of her soul. She seemed very young when it came to the ways of the world, yet she was both mysterious and tough. She intrigued him.

Closing his eyes, he clamped his mouth down over hers. Even though he was happy being there with Dakota, kissing her passionately, touching her tenderly, he was genuinely surprised when he began to mentally make comparisons between her and other women in his life.

Dakota was totally different from anyone in his past. She kept him curious. He was attracted to her personality, her sweet, shy demeanor, and her great sense of humor. How well she communicated with him was also on the list of positives, but rarely was his curiosity about her ever fulfilled. He'd have to consider that a negative, unfortunately.

Ethan held up both of Dakota's hands and kissed the back of each. "I feel like getting out. Are you up to a short stroll on the beach?"

Dakota faked a bout of shivers. "It's kind of chilly out there, don't you think?"

He held up his arms and flexed his

muscles. "These big boys wrapped around you will keep you heated up. You could also wear a warm jacket," he said, chuckling.

Dakota laughed. "A combination of those strong arms and a jacket just might work. I'll be right back." She got up and started toward the rear of her apartment.

Ethan silently thanked God for how painless it had been for him and Dakota to come together again, though it had been kind of awkward. He hoped there wouldn't be any more absences for them.

Ethan's arms provided her more comfort than warmth against the chilly air. They also made her feel safe. As the water lapped against the sandy shores, she watched and listened to the lulling sounds of nightfall. The quarter moon was high in the sky and the stars were shining brilliantly. The colorful neon signs on the boardwalk added a flashy exhilaration to the atmosphere. Dakota reached up and placed one of her hands over Ethan's, massaging it lightly. "Taking a walk was a nice idea."

He looked down into her eyes. "During the late evenings, I love walking on the beach. When I can't sleep, I go outdoors and run. You'd be surprised at the number of folks who jog late at night."

"I'm not astonished by much that goes on in and around L.A. after dark. Most of the beach cities come alive just before sunset. Look at all the couples out here tonight."

"Do you consider us a couple?" Ethan asked.

"Putting me on the spot, huh?"

"Not really. But I'd like an answer to my question."

"Then I'll give you one. When you stopped calling, I mulled over that a lot. I've thought of us as a couple."

Ethan was able to stop himself from jumping up and down and shouting with joy. "Are you still opposed to an exclusive relationship?"

She kicked away a small stone in her path. "I can tell you this much, you're the only person I go out with socially. I don't have close friends. I chat with classmates and coworkers, but I don't see them outside of classes or at work." If Ethan knew the kind of crazy schedule she had, he'd more than likely understand why she didn't have time to nurture friendships. And those who she'd once thought of as friends had betrayed her despite knowing about her and Danielle's losses.

"It seems like you have a hard time committing to an exclusive relationship. Am I right?"

She sighed hard. "Why is that type relationship so important to you?" Her tone was impatient.

"I don't want anyone dating you but me. That's as right to the point as I can get."

Dakota lifted an eyebrow. "People often talk of committing to a relationship. Then they go right out and do the exact opposite," she said, sounding disappointed. "Saying it doesn't make it so. Showing that you're committed is much better than simply saying it," she cited on a note of sadness.

Dakota's theory had Ethan thinking hard about what she'd said. It didn't take him long to realize it made a lot of sense. Saying it *didn't* make it so. "Are you saying we should watch what people do rather than listen to what they say?"

"A combination of both might work better. I've already told you that someone whom I believed was committed to me cheated with my best friend. I also mentioned how a couple of my girlfriends betrayed me. I'm sorry, but it's just not that easy to put a lot of faith in someone promising me a commitment."

Ethan didn't know if it was what she'd

said or how she'd said it that had made her position much clearer for him. She *had* been hurt badly. That much was crystal clear. From all indications, her wounds weren't healed yet. No matter how much he wanted to repair her shattered heart, it wasn't in his power. It wasn't like she hadn't mentioned her issues of trust.

Did Dakota think he would go back on his promise? When he'd told her they could dispense with talk of going exclusive, he'd meant it. Now he realized all he'd done was try to press her into committing to a one-on-one relationship with him.

Ethan abruptly stopped in his tracks and turned to Dakota. His hands cupped her face. "I owe you an apology. I remember what I promised you. You've called me on it before . . . and now I'm calling myself out. No more pressure from me about you making a commitment. Please give me another shot at this. I've failed twice already. Hopefully the third time will be the charm. I want to get it right."

Ethan kissed Dakota gently and then arduously.

She smiled to show him how much she approved of what he'd said. She was glad the pressure was off. She understood his wanting her to commit. In turn, she hopefully had been successful in getting him to understand that everyone promising commitment didn't always mean it. If she ever decided to commit to him, she would definitely live up to it. She had done it before. Although committing hadn't gotten her anything but hurt, she wasn't going to believe all men were created equal in cheating hearts.

At the end of the boardwalk, Ethan and Dakota turned around and headed back, feeling much better. They'd reached a greater degree of understanding. It was clearer to Ethan what she needed from him and he was dedicated to delivering the goods.

Ethan slung his arms around Dakota's shoulders and pulled her in closer. "This is one beautiful night and you're one beautiful woman. How could a guy ask for more?"

Dakota smiled. "Believe it or not, there are too many men who'd not only ask for more, but they'd also demand it. At the same time, they'd require nothing more from themselves."

"That's an interesting observation. How long *were* you with this guy who jerked you around?"

Her eyes widened. "Why'd you ask me that? Is the pain still obvious?"

"It is. I'm sorry you were so badly hurt."

"Me, too, but that's no reason for me to take it out on others. It seems to me I was involved with him for too long. Now it's imperative I let go of the pain and move on. It's a new day and my future is waiting on me." *Maybe even destiny.*

"I'm all for a new day." He bent his head to find pleasure in her sweet kiss. As their mouths united, he was completely run over with staggering excitement.

Feeling exhilarated from the walk on the beach, Dakota and Ethan strolled to the front entry of her apartment. After handing him the keys, she patiently waited for him to unlock the door. Using the remote on her key chain, he disarmed the alarm. Mission accomplished, he stepped aside, allowing her to precede him. He was so glad they were together, happy she'd let him come over. Maybe she was even ready to clear up for him the details behind Dan, the mystery man in her life. *Fat chance.*

"Is it okay if I fix us some coffee?" Ethan asked Dakota.

"Sure. I'll come in the kitchen with you."

Ethan made coffee while Dakota warmed in the toaster oven a couple of slices of homemade lemon pound cake she'd removed from the freezer. One of her class-mates had brought her the cake a few days ago. She'd eaten only one slice and had frozen the rest to enjoy at another time.

Dakota moved about the kitchen, thinking about the things they'd said to each other during their walk. The commitment issue had been settled. He now understood what he hadn't been able to get earlier. He had promised not to pressure her and she believed he'd keep his word this time. They had come to an amicable understanding, one they could both live with. Her smile caused her eyes to twinkle with the giddi-ness she felt. Something wonderful was go-ing to happen for them. She felt it in her spirit.

"Where're the spoons?"

Dakota pointed at the drawer where the everyday silverware was kept. She also had a set of sterling silverware that once be-longed to her parents, which had been a wedding present to them from her mother's parents.

Dakota went over to the table and poured two cups of hot coffee from the carafe. She then served the warm dessert on small glass cake plates. Overly eager for her to join him, he was happy when she finally sat down.

Ethan pinched off a piece of cake, popped

it into his mouth and swallowed. "How's your weekend shaping up? Have any free time?"

Even though Ethan hadn't given any indication that he wanted to spend time with her, it didn't stop Dakota from wishing and hoping. "Lots of errands and house cleaning during the day, but my evenings are free."

"I'd like us to get together over the weekend. How does that sound?" He gave her a beautiful smile.

"Very nice. Friday or Saturday?"

"Would you consider me a greedy man if I asked for both?"

"Both it is. What time?"

"I'll leave that up to you. Sooner is better, though, because time seems to fly when we're together. I wish I knew how to slow it down a bit."

"You know that's impossible. Harnessing time can't be done." Dakota's heart felt like it was bursting with passion. His flattering remarks had her soaring on a natural high.

"That doesn't stop me from wanting to try. When I'm with you, I feel alive. I feel like I can accomplish just about anything."

She knew what he meant. His comments mirrored her sentiments. "You can accomplish anything, with or without me."

"The thought of getting it done with you at my side is way more appealing." He leaned across the table and kissed her mouth. His heart began to race. Kissing her was good for him, great for his overall well-being.

Dakota responded ardently to Ethan's kisses. Her emotions were running high. She wasn't sure if she'd ever see him again, but he was here. She was ecstatic. She got up from her seat and stood right in front of him. "I want you to hold me. Your absence was pretty rough at times."

Ethan stood and put his arm around Dakota's shoulders, guiding her into the living room, where they sat down on the sofa. As she buried her face against his chest, tears fell from her eyes and her shoulders began to shake. His deep feelings for her washed over him like a tidal wave.

Stroking her arms tenderly, he whispered to her not to cry. Ethan lifted Dakota's chin and looked into her eyes. "What's wrong?"

Dakota hungrily covered Ethan's mouth with hers, kissing him passionately. She didn't want to talk. There was nothing wrong. Everything was right. All she wanted was to be held and touched by him. Although she'd had many ordeals in her lifetime, this was the first time in a long while she had a man to turn to.

With her hands trembling hard, Dakota lifted up Ethan's sweater and pulled it over his head. She heard his sharp intake of breath as she went for his T-shirt. Her breathing quickened as her palms roved over his broad chest. The feel of his warm, hard flesh excited her. Her mouth continued to work magic on his.

Dakota lifted her head and looked into his eyes. "I want you," she whispered. "I want you so much."

Ethan felt himself starting to lose control, yet he didn't think he should let the seduction go any further. She had been crying only a few moments ago. He didn't take advantage of vulnerable women.

Then Dakota's tongue coiled around his, flicking in and out of his mouth. The fiery stimulation caused his brain to go numb. His nipples suddenly became the focus of her attention, as she manipulated each with her fingertips and then with her tongue. Dakota set his body ablaze.

"Dakota, we should . . ."

Her mouth tenderly meshed with his, silencing him instantly. She didn't want to listen to reason, nor did she want him to talk her out of what she'd already made up her mind to do. Dakota wanted to make love to Ethan. The granitelike hardness of his sex let her know he wanted her, too. She didn't know if he loved her, but she was madly in love with him. That was a good enough reason for her to give him her all.

Dakota stripped out of her blouse, nearly popping off the last button in her haste to disrobe. The lacy black-and-white Swiss dotted bra with see-through cups was sexy. She stood briefly. As she slid her jeans down over her hips, she watched him stare at the bikinis with the same lacy and dotted pattern as her bra. She stretched out on the sofa.

Ethan's dark eyes continued to drink in her beautiful body. Her flesh looked silky and soft. To find out if he was right, he lay alongside her on the sofa, allowing his hands to slowly move up and down her thighs. She was hot to the touch, feverishly moist. Making love to Dakota wasn't something he'd planned, but he couldn't deny how she made him feel.

Working loose the top button on Ethan's jeans wasn't as easily accomplished by her, but she got the job done. Slowly, in a tantalizing way, she went to work on the metal zipper. Dakota's hand slid inside Ethan's silk briefs and gently fondled his manhood. His sex grew even more rigid.

Tenderly catching her lower lip between his teeth, he sucked on it. His mouth fully claimed hers, their tongues engaging in a heated exchange.

Dakota made sure her eyes connected dead-on with his. She smiled softly, licking her top lip provocatively. Her long lashes fluttered and then slowly lowered again. She'd never before been so bold as to seduce a man, yet she had no desire to turn back.

Ethan's eyes locked in on Dakota's pretty face. Holding his gaze steady, he lowered one of her bra straps, placing buttery-soft kisses on her creamy shoulder. His mouth moved downward. Tilting her head back slightly, he brushed his lips against her throat. Using the tip of his tongue, he left a line of moist fire up and down her neck, his breath white-hot against her flesh.

Hungry for the sweet taste of Dakota, Ethan sought out her mouth again and again. Each kiss was more intense than the previous one. Never in his life had he wanted anyone the way he desired the woman beneath him.

Taking his own sweet time, Ethan made an art form of stripping Dakota bare. He twirled around on his finger the bikinis and bra before tossing aside her sexy unmentionables. His mouth and tongue began to feverishly explore every inch of her body, tasting, teasing and torching her tender flesh.

Now that she was removing his briefs, his mind focused on the soft feel of her delicate hands and gently probing fingers.

Dakota inserted her tongue into the center of Ethan's navel. He gasped with wantonness, her name right on the tip of his tongue. He kept his cool, but all he really wanted to do was scream out. The lady had been successful in getting a three-alarm fire started.

Once he'd donned protection, Ethan shifted around on the sofa until he had Dakota flat on her back. He lowered himself down onto her body. Her legs parted and then wrapped high up around his waist. A sudden explosion rocked his world as her bare skin singed his. If just the coming together of their naked flesh was a TNT experience, he could only imagine what might happen once he was inside her. Still, he wasn't in a hurry. He was enjoying every delicious moment.

Kissing Dakota was a favorite display of affection for Ethan. Their mouths seemed to align perfectly and she tasted sweet as honey. Her full mouth gave him so much pleasure. The kisses had intensified beyond his greatest expectations. "I need you. I want you, Dakota."

Looking up at him, smiling, she slowly dragged her tongue across his bottom lip. "Take me. I'm yours."

Stopping at intervals to give Dakota a chance to adjust to his thickness, Ethan nipped at her lower lip, suckled her breasts and nipples and kissed her ripe mouth. All the while, he tenderly inched his way inside the beautiful, sexy woman lying beneath him. She gasped softly throughout the entry process, pleasurable intakes of breath.

Dakota's hands gently stroked Ethan's back and buttocks as he delved deeper into her inner sanctum. As her fingertips played up and down his spine, she felt every fiery stroke. It felt good to have him tenderly yet wildly manipulating her inner treasures. The pleasure she felt was immense, mind-blowing, yet his touch was warm and loving. He made her feel as if pleasuring her was more important than meeting his own needs.

As Ethan plunged in and out of her moist canal, Dakota's head moved from side to side. Her desire for more of him caused her to lift up her lower body to meet his deep thrusts. The moist kisses he rained all over her face and neck made her feel special. His tongue flicking in and out of her ears made her squirm all over the place. Making love to Ethan in the flesh was much better than the sessions she'd imagined.

Quickly, Ethan rolled off her and got to his feet. Lifting her into his arms, he carried her through the house and into the bedroom, keeping up the hot and heavy foreplay.

After Ethan laid Dakota atop the mattress, she pulled down Ethan's head, looking into his eyes. "I'm committed to you, to us. I love you, Ethan Robinson, with all my heart and soul."

Ethan felt a rush of latent relief. Dakota confessing her love to him had knocked the wind out of him. Her loving him was a dream fulfilled. Destiny *had* arrived. His eyes filled with moisture. "I love you, too. I'm glad we've arrived at the same place. I've been in love with you a long time now."

Climbing into bed alongside her, he lifted her again, holding her up slightly above him. Slowly, he drew her down over his manhood. *We're in love.* It was awesome.

Unable to stop herself, Dakota screamed out, spurred on by passion. To stop another outburst, she bit down on her lower lip. Even that didn't stop the roiling heat from vibrating inside her body.

225

As the couple's steamy, sweaty flesh merged fervently, time and time again, there was a rhythm to the way he drew her up and down on his rigid sex. Picking up the pace, his hands tightly gripping her hips, he guided her wild, bucking motions. The thrashing about in the bed continued to intensify. Each confessed their love aloud.

Unable to hold back a minute longer, the couple united together in an earth-shattering release, totally spent, utterly fulfilled. With him still inside her, she leaned forward, resting her head on his broad chest. It was clear to both that they were in love.

Ethan massaged Dakota's back. "You *are* wonderful, you know. I've never been this happy. Sorry about how I treated you before," he said sincerely. He hoped his remarks would open up some dialogue about the place where he'd followed her to and why she'd gone there.

"I understood your being upset with me. I had an emergency to tend to, nothing more or less. Missing you so much helped me see just how ready I am for you and me."

Disappointment covered how Ethan felt. It seemed as if she planned to cling to her secrets. Deciding it was best not to dwell on something he couldn't change, he repositioned himself in bed and pulled her into his arms. "Do you want to shower?"

"Are you joining me?"

"You want me to?"

"Wouldn't want it any other way."

He beamed at her. "Let me just lie here with you another minute or two." He wanted to bask in her warmth and hold her close. "Then we'll take that hot shower together. Can I talk you into letting me spend the night?"

"I was hoping you'd want to stay. But I have to leave home early tomorrow." She laughed inwardly, wondering what he'd think of her cold showers.

"That makes two of us." He kissed the tip of her nose. "I'll make sure you get a lot of rest, but it'll be hard for me to sleep next to you and contain the excitement I always feel when I'm with you. I'm glad tomorrow is Friday. I'm looking forward to the weekend."

"Me, too, but we'll both need our rest to tackle work tomorrow."

"You're right about that. I'll do my best."

She gave him a doubtful look. "I'm sure you will."

Dakota turned on the shower and then rapidly moved behind Ethan. As the first blast of cold water splashed over his body, he yelped, hopping all around in the shower. He hastily reached for the controls to try to change the water temperature. After fumbling around with the stainless steel dials for several seconds, he finally got some hot water to flow through.

The look on Ethan's face was priceless to Dakota. She couldn't help laughing at his comical reaction. The cold water had been quite a shock to him. "Sorry about that. I guess I should've told you I take cold showers." She laughed heartily.

Ethan eyed her with skepticism. "You planned this, didn't you? Come here, you little vixen." He reached for her, wrapping her in his arms. "That was mean-spirited."

"Maybe it was." She chuckled. "But I'd do it again, just to see your reaction. You were hilarious. You've never taken a cold shower before?"

"Well, yeah, maybe in high school and college. I like my water steaming. And don't you forget it."

She kissed him gently on the mouth. "I won't forget. I promise."

"Okay." He kissed her forehead. "Now on to better things."

Ethan sat on the floor of the tub, drawing

Dakota onto his lap, so that she straddled him. As he kissed her with wild abandon, his hands twisted up in her hair. He loved the magic she brought to his life. As the warm water pelted down over them, he suckled her nipples and touched the most sensitive parts of her body.

Dakota loved the touch of his hands, experts in manipulation, bringing her pleasure. Completely losing her mind in his kiss, it was the first time in a long while she was able to totally lock out the everyday challenges. Ready for him to be inside her, she lifted up slightly and began to lower her intimate treasures down onto his manhood. Throwing her head back, she laughed.

Ethan held her head back. "What's so funny?"

"We can't do this right now."

He looked puzzled. "Why not?"

"We don't have a condom."

Ethan laughed, too. "Talk about lousy timing." His expression quickly turned serious. "I'm sorry. Let me go get protection. I'll be right back."

She refused to let him get up, seductively moving her buttocks against his naked flesh. "Not yet. There's more than one way to skin a cat. We can save the condom for when we get back to the bedroom."

Ethan grinned. "You *are* a little minx, aren't you? I love the naughty girl in you."

CHAPTER 10

Awakening in the middle of the night, Dakota turned over in her bed. Not used to anyone sleeping with her, she bumped right into Ethan's nude body. It startled her momentarily. Then she smiled, recalling the delicious sins they'd already indulged in. Thinking about the foreplay in the shower made her temperature soar.

Propping up her head on one elbow, she looked down at Ethan. He was beautiful, inside and out, even asleep. Not wanting to disturb him kept her from crushing his silky hair between her fingers.

As she turned over to try to go back to sleep, Ethan pulled her down into his arms, ravishing her mouth. As his tongue curved around hers, he moaned softly. "I only had two condoms. But that doesn't mean you have to do without." In one swift motion, he turned her on her back. Starting with her neck, he licked and laved his way down to the entry of her intimate secrets.

The tip of Ethan's tongue flicked wildly at the entry of Dakota's secret treasures and she nearly lifted off, heaven-bound. With her breath caught in a myriad of tangles, she arced upward each time he tenderly tasted the soft flesh between her legs.

Nothing quite like this over-the-top was in her realm of experience. The trembling within her inner core made her tug hard on his hair.

Ethan continued to devour Dakota. His tongue moved faster and faster now, working her completely over, as though he knew she was burning hot, ready for that tumultuous release. She fell into ecstasy.

The alarm clock awakened Dakota. Opening one eye, she looked over at the digital numbers. *Six-fifteen, Friday morning.* She looked over at the side of the bed where Ethan had slept all night long. He wasn't there. She then spotted her purse in the chair where her clothes were folded neatly. It was obvious he had picked up her things from off the living room floor, right where their lovemaking escapades had begun.

Groaning with displeasure, Dakota rolled over onto her back, wondering where Ethan was. As she thought about Danielle, she leaped out of bed and ran over to her purse. Grabbing her cell phone, she got back into bed and quickly put a call into the facility.

"Hi, it's Dakota. How's my precious Danni this morning?"

"Danielle is just fine, Dakota," Nurse Compton said. "She had a good night, but she's not awake yet. I'll let her know you called."

"Thank you. When I called into the nurses' station last night, I was told she was resting well. I'll be up there at my usual time."

"Okay, Dakota. We'll see you later. Take care."

After getting to her feet, Dakota put away her phone. She then hurried into the bathroom to shower. As the memories of the past evening lit up her mind and warmed her heart, her smile was sweetly wicked. So many wonderful memories had occurred. The foreplay they'd indulged in in the shower also earned a high ranking.

Dakota hurried and brushed her teeth and then swished around in her mouth a capful of Scope. She peeked out the bathroom door to see if Ethan had come back to the bedroom. He still wasn't around. In the interest of time, she couldn't wait any longer. She stepped into the shower and turned on the cold water, momentarily bracing herself for the big chill to pass through her. Perhaps the cold shower was the reason he hadn't showed up. Dakota laughed, recalling his hilarious performance last evening.

Wearing a pair of red jeans and a white shirt, Dakota quickly made her way to the front of her apartment, calling out Ethan's name. The nonresponse puzzled her. She continued on toward the kitchen, hoping to find him there. A delicious coffee aroma was in the air. Sure she'd find him slaving over the stove, she giggled, speeding up.

As Dakota glanced over at the table, her smile rapidly turned to a frown. An envelope with her name on it was propped against the napkin holder. It seemed ominous.

They'd made love for the first time — several incredible times . . . and all she had of him the morning after was a handwritten note.

Before braving the read, she poured a cup of coffee in her personalized mug he'd left beside the coffeemaker. Deciding the java was too hot to drink, she set it aside. After retrieving the envelope, she rapidly ripped it open. The happy face Ethan had drawn at the top of the letter caused Dakota's smile to return.

Sorry, but I had to leave earlier than I had anticipated. You were sleeping peacefully, so I just left the alarm clock alone. You agreed to spend time with me today and Saturday, so I'll see you this evening. We both confessed our love in the heat of passion, but I meant it. I hope you did, too. I love you.

Dakota read the note again and again, strong emotions sweeping through her each time. "I really meant it, Ethan. I'm deeply in love with you, always and forever."

Dakota was driving toward her destination when her cell phone rang. She pressed in the button on her Bluetooth to begin communication. California had passed a new law nearly a year ago: no cell phone usage without a hands-free device. "Hello."

"Sorry I didn't see you before I left this morning. Things are already hectic here at the job. Are we still on for this evening?"

"Seven-thirty is good for me," she said. "What about you?"

"I can make it then," he assured her, sounding happy. "Want to go out to dinner?"

"I'd like to have a quiet time at home. I'll fix something or we can order takeout."

"Don't go to too much trouble. I'll see you this evening. I love you."

"I love you, too," she sang out. "See you later." Dakota clicked off.

Was tonight the time for her to tell Ethan all about Danielle?

The fear of hearts becoming compromised, only to be broken, frightened Dakota. She was so in love with Ethan, but if he couldn't accept Danielle, it was over for them. Her not telling him about her sister from the beginning could very well produce the same effect. Just the thought of that made her sick in the stomach.

Dakota pulled her car into the parking lot of Licensed to Thrill. She hated going inside, but she had to pull her shift. She had thought of calling in sick, but she didn't earn sick time, so she'd lose wages. Four hours was all she had to put in, but there were instances when it felt like she was doing hard time.

Instant relief flooded over Luke when he heard Persia's sexy voice. He sat down on the sofa and propped his feet on the hassock. "How's my good buddy today?"

"I've had better days, but I always seem

to make it through. How are you?"

"I'm okay."

"Are you still there, friend?" Persia asked.

"Sorry, my thought process got jammed up. But I'm back now. Tell me this, Ms. Persia, how many phone calls have you received so far today and how many do you wish hadn't happened?"

Persia was tickled by his question. "It's been slow so far. The few calls I did get were kind of interesting. I receive a host of 'wanting to get to know you' calls and also those from guys who are new to the area. You'd be surprised at how many men call here thinking this is a dating service. I actually feel bad when I have to clue them in. They seem upset when I tell them it's not, but they keep on talking."

"Your calls do run the gamut, don't they?"

Persia noticed that Luke's voice wasn't as upbeat as usual. If he wasn't depressed, his tone came across that way. "You can say that again," Persia said glibly.

"Your coworkers, are you friends with any of them?"

"I chat with a couple ladies here during working hours, but we don't get together outside the job," she remarked, a ring of disappointment in her tone.

"Have your coworkers ever told you why

they got into this business."

"Sure. It's pretty unanimous. Money. Like I told you before, most of the women who work here have been referred by other employees. It's rare for someone to just apply for a position here, unless they were PSOs somewhere else."

"Are there a lot of college students working there?"

"Around four to one. We talk about bettering ourselves through education. But some women graduate and continue to work here."

"Why's that?"

"The money! Everything around here has to do with finances. Some women try their best to make the job fun, so they don't get down on themselves. Then, there are those like me, the ones who hate it with a passion," she said sadly.

"Are guys employed there?"

"A few companies hire guys to work the lines for women who are interested in calling in to have men talk sexy to them. But women really don't phone in to sex lines as much as men. The males in the industry prefer stripping and dancing to earn their paychecks, especially the private party scene. And many of them do what you do. Money is endless, depending on what you're willing to do. I'm sure you know all about that."

"You said it, not me," he remarked with a chuckle. "Do you think you'll quit once you get your degree?"

"I know I will, Luke."

"That certainly came out as a matter of fact. How can you be so sure?"

"I am sure. I know how to keep my eye on the prize. This isn't something I just do for extra cash. My livelihood depends on it right now."

"I wonder who I'll talk to you once you retire from this gig? We get along so well. I think we would make great friends."

"I thought we'd discussed that. It will never happen. Trust me on that."

"Persia, anything is possible."

"How much money do adult films really pay?" she asked, changing topic.

"You asked me that before. Like I said, it all depends on what an actor is willing to do. I make gobs of money for one picture. It wasn't always that way. I recall a time when I got less than a thousand for a job. Of course it didn't entail much. But I'm in demand now. My agent could book me a gig every day if that's what I wanted. I'm real choosy now. Every element has to be just right and I have to actually like my costar."

"Do you star with men or just women?"

"Just women, baby. I'm only into the ladies."

"Talk about matter of fact. You didn't pull any punches on that one," Persia said, laughing softly.

"I rarely pull punches, sweetheart. I just tell it like it is."

Dakota smiled at Danielle as she accepted the box the McDonald's Happy Meal had come in. Big sister was pleased to see that all the French fries and the hamburger had been eaten. Nothing but the trash was left inside. "You want your apple pie now?"

Danielle rubbed her stomach. "I'm full. Can I eat it later?"

"Okay. I'll put it over here on the table. Are you finished with your drink?"

Danielle shook her head. "I'll try to finish it." She knew Dakota didn't like her to waste food and drink, so she tried to consume everything she was given.

"You don't have to drink it if you're too full." Dakota walked across the room and lifted the cup off the nightstand. "It's practically empty anyway. I'll toss the rest."

"I can drink it later, Kota."

"It'll be watered down by then."

"My tummy *is* full."

"I can see that." Dakota sat on the side of the bed and gently massaged Danielle's stomach. "What do you want to do for the rest of my visit?"

"Will you read to me?"

"Sure. What story do you want?"

Danielle pointed at the children's Bible her sister had given her as a Christmas gift. "When Jesus fed all the people." She looked up at her sister, curiosity floating in her eyes. "Why didn't they get sick like me? Jesus fed the people fish."

It *was* a legitimate question, especially after what she'd gone through with the allergic reaction. "Let me find the Sermon on the Mount." Dakota walked over to the bookshelf and removed the colorful hardback book. She then went back and reclaimed her seat.

"First off, I'm sure you recall Dr. Alexander and Nurse Compton explaining to you that the iodine was the problem. Second, everyone's not allergic to fish, sweetie. You are now, but you haven't always been. It's something that cropped up out of the blue. I know how much you love seafood, but you just can't have it anymore."

Danielle giggled. "That's why I want you

to read about it."

After lying across the bottom of Danielle's bed, Dakota shifted her body around until she found a comfortable position. Her emotions burgeoned every time she read a story from the Bible, a book chock-full of miracles. Today was no different.

Dakota considered Danielle as one of God's miracles, too.

The fried chicken and French fries Dakota had picked up on her way home had been covered with aluminum foil and put in an oven set for warming only. She then refrigerated the sides of coleslaw and macaroni salad.

Because Dakota had time enough to take a hot bath, she walked into the bathroom and turned on both the hot and cold water, testing it with her fingers until the right temperature was achieved. Liquid bubbles and bath salts were added before she stripped out of her clothing. Standing nude in front of the mirror, she brushed her hair into a ponytail, twisting the hair around and then pinning it up securely. Locating her bathrobe came next. She spotted it on top of the dirty clothes hamper, within easy reach of the tub.

It was unusual for her to take a hot bath

when she was having company, but a cold shower wasn't going to achieve what she needed. The steaming water and bath salts relaxed her muscles and the frothy bubbles soothed her skin.

Nesting her head back on the bath pillow, Dakota closed her eyes, her mind drifting toward thoughts of Ethan. She wished she didn't think about him so much, but he occupied even the dusty corners of her mind. She laughed at her silliness.

What could possibly be more pleasant than lying around, reminiscing about all of their wonderful, scintillating escapades? Not a thing. It made her feel good to know she fulfilled Ethan's sexual desires. The man had no problem letting her know what she did for him in bed. As for her, he kept her body hot and out of control.

Ethan poured pink lemonade into glasses filled with ice, while Dakota retrieved the food from the oven and refrigerator. He had also helped her set the table. She had fallen asleep in the tub and had just barely finished dressing. Her hair was still pinned up when the doorbell had rung.

The black-and-silver Oakland Raider sweatshirt looked good on her. Instead of oversize, the shirt was roomy yet fit her very well. He was flattered that she'd chosen to wear the gift he'd purchased for her. The black jeans were a perfect fit, highlighting her alluring figure.

Dakota set the bread basket on the table, filled with delicious biscuits, buttery and flaky. "We're all set now. We can sit down and eat."

Ethan pulled out her chair. Once she was seated, he took a chair. He reached over and took hold of her hand and passed a simple but humble blessing.

As a breast man, Ethan chose the biggest one out of the eight pieces of chicken. He also helped himself to a plump wing. "Spicy?"

"Spicy. I recall that's how you like your chicken."

"I love a woman who listens. Touché. You must be tired if you went out like a light while in the tub. Your reasoning for taking cold showers makes more sense now."

"I am sooo tired. With school and work, my plate stays full."

"We've got that in common, but we do what we have to," he admitted. "I hope you won't be too tired to attend the California African-American Museum Gala with me next weekend. Sorry I'm so late asking, but I was given tickets by one of my colleagues only today. Tickets were sold out for this special event when I tried to purchase two. It didn't make sense to mention it because it appeared there was no chance of us attending."

Attending the gala with Ethan was so appealing to Dakota. If the dress code called for fancy clothes, everything in her closet fell way short. She didn't own a stitch of formal or semiformal attire. "I won't be able to attend." She looked down at the floor for a moment. "Afraid I don't have anything to wear to dress-up affairs. And I can't tell you how much I hate admitting it."

The gala was a black-tie event, Ethan knew. That she was troubled by her clothing dilemma had him trying to find a solution. He could offer to purchase appropriate apparel for her, but feared the suggestion might be offensive. And he wasn't one to get in the way of a person's dignity. "Maybe we can attend next year. It's only the fourth year for the museum to hold a gala."

The yen to attend the prestigious event with Ethan was powerful. She saw it as a great opportunity. As she thought about the emergency money, she undoubtedly knew there was enough to buy a dress, shoes and accessories. She had purchased two pieces of luggage out of it and a few other personal items, but she hadn't used any funds on herself before Oakland.

"Think you can give me a couple days to figure out what I'd need to purchase?"

Ethan nodded. "The tickets aren't going anywhere." He paused a moment, carefully thinking about his next comment. "I have Macy's and Nordstrom's credit cards. If you want to use one, you can, and pay me back as your finances dictate."

An emotional lump formed in her throat, causing her to swallow hard. "That was very kind of you. I'll give it some thought."

Ethan was surprised. "Good. I'd love to go shopping with you. Maybe I can help pick out your outfit." He knew he had put himself out on a fragile limb. Walking a tightrope was always risky business, but her answer had provided him a safety net. He hadn't offended her. He was happy about that. "Actor Dennis Haysbert is acting as Program Host and Muhammad Ali will be presented a Lifetime Achievement Award."

That statement drew a soft whistle from Dakota. She was impressed by the host and the award recipient. "I love both men. I *do* want to go." She took a deep breath. "You know what? I accept your invitation."

Ethan didn't think Dakota was half as excited as he was. "You just made my day, lady. If you need help shopping or any funds, let me know."

"Want a cup of coffee, Ethan?"

"That'd be nice. But I'll get the coffee-maker going, Dakota. You want some?"

"I'll fix it. Go on in the living room and relax. While the coffee is brewing, I'll load the dishwasher and wipe off everything."

The expression on her face seemed to tell Ethan not to protest. She had recently told him she liked cooking for him and tending to his needs. As much as he'd like to help her make the coffee and clean up the kitchen, something told him to do just what she'd asked. Her easygoing ways made her a delight.

Walking over to the counter, he took her in his arms and kissed her thoroughly. "I miss you too easily, so don't make me wait too long."

Her forefinger traced his forehead to the deep dimple in his chin. "You won't get a chance to miss me." She kissed the tip of his nose.

Ethan kissed Dakota again and then sauntered out the room.

Ethan rushed over to Dakota. Taking the metal serving tray from her hands, he set it on the coffee table and returned to his seat on the sofa. She sat down beside him. Next she poured steaming coffee from the carafe into two ceramic mugs.

The soft music streaming from the television speakers was popular rhythm and blues tunes, slow songs from a variety of years. Ethan had tuned the digital cable box to one of the music channels he loved to listen to when at home.

Lifting his cup, he held it up to Dakota's lips. "Make it sweet for me. Blow on it and then taste it."

She laughed at his request before doing just so. This was the first time anyone had made her an official taste tester. She loved that Ethan had chosen her to be his personal sampler, just another of his sweet gestures toward her.

Ethan took a small sip, pausing a second before taking a swig. "Ah, just the way I like it. You made it taste so good, lady."

Dakota put a sliver of pie on a fork and blew on it just as she'd done the coffee, though it wasn't nearly as hot. Then she offered up the pie to Ethan, their eyes connecting steamily. Staring into her orbs, he slowly ate the pie from the fork. This exchange went on between the couple for the next few minutes. As they ate the pie and drank the coffee from each other's cups and utensils, their passion continued to mount.

Dakota opened the first couple of buttons on Ethan's shirt, sliding her hands through the opening. She loved the soft feel of his chest hairs, which were thick and plentiful. Her mouth feasted on his while rolling his hardened nipple between her thumb and forefinger. She liked to make him moan, gasp and whisper her name.

Working loose the top button on his jeans and slipping them off over his hips and feet was much easier for Dakota than it was the first time, because he guided her hands, whispering to her where and how to touch him. This time it was Dakota who reached for his wallet to remove a condom.

Once Dakota had the latex circle in her hand, he'd recovered from the shock she'd put him in. Every day was a new surprise from her . . . and he liked them all. Ethan liked having her take the initiative.

Outlining Ethan's lips with her tongue was as thrilling to her as it was to him. The tip of her tongue teased his ears, inner and outer. "I want you. Do you want me?"

"Badly." He suckled her lower lip. "Undress for me. I want to watch as you bare your body. Give me a show I won't ever forget."

Dakota threw her head back and laughed

wickedly. "It's a show you want, huh? Well, let's see what we can do about that." She dialed back slightly the volume on the music channel. When she heard Chris Brown and Jordin Sparks singing "No Air," she thought it was the perfect song to enact a slow strip tease.

In slow motion, Dakota began to come out of her clothes in dramatic fashion, earning his rapt attention, taking advantage of his desire to have her. The first item to go was her top. Leaving her bra in place, she slowly wiggled the jeans down over her hips.

As though she were modeling, she made several dramatic poses, her tongue circling the tip of her fingernail. Pushing her hands up through her hair, until it was all over her head, she eyed him intently, flirtatiously. She hadn't ever felt this uninhibited before and it felt good. Visualizing some of the scripts she'd read at work helped her to enact a highly erotic exhibition for Ethan.

Beyoncé's "If I Were a Boy," one of Ethan's favorite songs, sluiced smoothly through the air. Getting up from the sofa, he pulled Dakota into his arms and engaged her in a seductive slow dance. As they swayed to the music, completely nude, his rock-hard manhood pressed against her thigh made her desire him in the worst way.

He lifted her and her legs went around his waist.

Kissing Dakota deeply, passionately, Ethan lifted her slightly higher. Gently, he made his way inside her. As his pulsating sex became one with her inner treasures, she totally lost every ounce of self-discipline. The musical rhythms their bodies created in unison was purely original. While making daring love, they danced their way deeper into each other's hearts.

CHAPTER 11

Stretched out on her bed, Dakota picked up the bills and counted them a third time. There was enough cash to get everything she needed, but she was still scared to use the emergency money in case problems arose. She also knew it would take her a good while to rebuild the funds.

The phone rang. Continuing to count the money wasn't going to change the amount, she knew. Stretching her arm over to the nightstand, she picked up the receiver. "Hello."

"Hi, Dakota, it's Charlene. How're you doing and what're you up to?"

Surprised was not the right word for what Dakota felt at hearing Maxwell's girlfriend on the other end. They'd never had a one-on-one conversation during group outings, let alone over the phone. Ethan must've given her the phone number.

"Sorry if I sent you into shock. You probably can't believe I'm calling."

"It *did* throw me, but it's really nice to hear from you. I'm just getting ready to go out shopping this morning."

"Ethan told Max and me he'd invited you to the museum gala. We're also attending. We've gone all three years. Where do you plan to shop?"

There was no way Dakota was telling her man's friend that she frequented consignment shops. She wasn't ashamed of it, but she didn't know if Charlene would get it. According to Ethan, Charlene's family was wealthy. "I'm heading to the Galleria in Torrance. Depending on the time, I may even hit Del Amo Mall."

"Listen, I rarely pay a lot of money on a dress for just one night. I know several great consignment shops located in Beverly Hills and Bel Air. We can buy obscenely expensive clothing and accessories for next to nothing. What do you think?"

"That you're onto something." Dakota laughed inwardly, sorry if she'd misjudged Charlene. "I'm no stranger to consignments shops." It felt good to Dakota to be herself.

"Great! I can be there in about thirty or forty minutes. I have your address."

Charlene's last statement suddenly made Dakota wary. *Had Ethan set up this little shopping spree? Maybe he did believe she really needed help in choosing the right attire.*

A glance at the clock showed nine-thirty. Most places didn't open until ten. Unsure of how to turn down this invitation, especially after showing some enthusiasm, she decided not to. Maybe she *could* use a little help in choosing appropriate attire. Two heads were always better than one, Dakota conceded. "I'll be ready when you get here."

"See you soon, Dakota," Charlene sang out.

Dakota hung up the phone but continued to lie across the bed, wondering if she was about to walk into a disastrous situation. She would know soon enough.

"First Impression," Dakota read aloud from the sign posted on the quaint little shop, wondering if the name lived up to what was sold inside. As she waited for Charlene, who was rearranging things in her trunk to ensure she had room for her purchases, excitement mounted in Dakota. Charlene let Dakota know that she planned to shop until she dropped. The thought of her two or three packages compared to Charlene's mountain of shopping bags made Dakota laugh.

Charlene rushed toward Dakota and

looped her arm through hers. "Let's get it on," Charlene enthused. "I do this all the time, but each spree is like a first-time high for me. I love shopping that much."

Amused by Charlene's animation, Dakota's eyes were stretched wide, shining with glee. Charlene acted like someone on speed, definitely pumped up. If they didn't get inside the shop right away, Dakota felt like she'd die from the anticipation.

An older lady came up to Charlene and hugged her, gushing niceties all over the place. "Good to see you again, Char. I see you brought a guest." She turned to Dakota and hugged her enthusiastically and greeted her like she'd known her forever. "I'm Mamie Childress, the owner. Welcome to First Impression."

Dakota was surprised by all the fuss the owner had made over her but was also warmed up by it. "Nice to meet you, Ms. Childress. You have quite a place here."

"You haven't seen the half of it, honey. Make yourself at home and enjoy your shopping experience." She pointed to an arched doorway. "There are refreshments in the other room. Charlene knows the ropes. This is a favorite hangout for her."

Racks and racks of clothing, suits, dresses and slacks lined three of four walls. Metal shoe racks, sorted by size, stood against the remaining wall. In the very center of the room, several long tables, decorated to impress, held all kinds of fine lingerie, sweaters, purses, jewelry, belts, sunglasses and a host of other fabulous merchandise.

Dakota immediately realized that First Impression was very different from any shop she'd ever patronized. Just the number of items for sale was one of the vast differences. The quality of the items was nothing short of exquisite, fashioned by top-notch designers. The shop did live up to its name. Her first impression was a great one.

Charlene came up to Dakota. "Is this place fantastic or what?"

"I'm totally impressed. It's first-class. Thanks for bringing me here."

"You're welcome. I'm happy to have your company. None of my friends shop with me anymore. I suspect I'd better buy in moderation today or I'll lose you, too."

Dakota laughed. "I'm not so sure about that. I like to shop, too, but . . ." She let her sentence trail off. There was no reason to announce her financial inability to shop. Taking care of her responsibilities was more important than buying clothes and shopping for things she didn't really need. Still, she imagined it would be nice.

To try to ease the awkwardness of the moment, Charlene grabbed hold of a flowing black gown. The sexy dress had sheer sleeves and bodice, dotted with black seed pearls and silvery-black sequins. "This has your name written all over it, Dakota. Why don't you try it on?"

Dakota read the Dolce & Gabbana label. She whistled lowly. Much to her stunned surprise, the original cost of the dress had been slashed down to bare bones. She could actually afford it, without filing for bankruptcy. "I will try it on." *It's my size and it definitely fits my purse strings.* Dakota shouted out her shoe size when she was asked.

Minutes after Dakota had installed herself in the small dressing room, Charlene brought to her several other gorgeous dresses to try on. Some of the labels included Oscar de la Renta, Prada, Bebe and Donna Karan. She had also picked out a pair of sequined Pierre Hardy peep-toe heels.

Dakota emerged from the dressing room for Charlene to voice her opinion.

Spotting the three-way mirror, she walked over to it and surveyed the dress from every angle. It was a magnificent creation, accentuating her gentle curves, showing enough cleavage to draw attention and to also incite Ethan's desire.

The beautiful woman who stared back at her was a virtual stranger, a happy-looking, contented one. She couldn't believe how well she cleaned up. Thoughts of her senior prom dress came to mind, the only other time she'd worn a full-length gown. She had been in awe of her looks that night, too. Smiling back at the stunning woman who'd been transformed by elegant attire and love, tears filled Dakota's eyes.

The formal-length dress fit Dakota as if it was tailored especially for her. Although they planned to go to other places she was already sold on this black beauty. Besides, she might not find something this perfect for her elsewhere, mainly the price. A bird in the hand was worth two in the bush, Dakota reminded herself. She could afford the dress and the shoes and still have a good bit of money left over. She'd need hosiery and jewelry, but those costs were manageable.

Dakota's mind was made up until Mamie Childress handed her a hot red dress designed by Diane von Furstenberg fashioned in a glittery silk crepe. "I believe this is your color. Your warm ginger complexion and Valentine red is a great combination."

Dakota was speechless for several seconds. The red gown did it for her on every level imaginable. Discreetly, she looked at the price tag. It was also within her realm of possibilities. She looked at herself in the mirror again. The black dress was a work of art on her body. "I'm fearful of trying on the red one 'cause I'll have to make a choice."

Charlene walked over to Dakota and squeezed her fingers. "You owe it to yourself to try it on. If you're short on cash, we can work something out." She winked at Dakota in a knowing way. "Both of these dresses are must-haves. Of course, we first have to see how the red one fits, but I've got a hunch it's also ideal for you."

Believing Charlene was absolutely right, Dakota hurried back into the dressing room. Her hands trembled as she took off one dress and carefully slipped into another.

The slightly ruffled neckline featured in the front and back of the dress was striking and provocative. The flowing gown was low-cut, with thin straps that crisscrossed. This moment was like a dream. She felt like a model on a runway.

Looking for advice from Charlene and Mamie, Dakota strolled out of the cubicle and stepped back over to the mirror. "Ladies, what do you think?"

They responded with loud gasps.

Mamie took a hold of Dakota's hand. "They're both perfect for you, but if you must choose between the two, the red gown gets my vote."

"I feel the same way," said Charlene. "But you should have both. Our group attends many formal events, especially during the upcoming Thanksgiving, Christmas and New Year's Eve holidays." How to see that she didn't miss out on a great opportunity had Charlene wondering if she'd be out of line or even stepping over it if she insisted on helping Dakota own both dresses.

Disappearing back into the dressing room, Dakota stared at her stunning image in the mirror while trying to make up her mind. If the black dress was a work of art, the elegant gown she had on was a red hot zinger. She never knew she could look so beautiful. As her thoughts zipped to Danielle, she wondered which one she would like the best. Red was her sister's favorite color. The red gown had to be the one.

Dakota returned the dresses to the padded hangers before stepping out of the dressing room. She then held up the red one. "Hands down, this is the one."

■ ■ ■ ■

The ladies went to three other consignment shops before they'd decided on having lunch together. Charlene had made quite a few acquisitions for herself. Just as she had predicted, her trunk was pretty full. Dakota was just plain tired, understanding why Charlene had a hard time keeping shopping buddies; the girl was an addicted shopper.

Dakota was surprised to see Maxwell seated at the table in Friday's. She bumped Charlene with her shoulder. "Did you know Maxwell would be here?"

"Of course I did. We've been communicating by cell all morning long."

"That explains your phone ringing every few minutes. If I had my car, I'd go on home. I'm sure you two can do lunch without me." No sooner than the words left her mouth did Ethan take a seat across from Maxwell. Dakota looked at Charlene, eyebrows raised. "Did you set this up?"

"Only with the finest man alive, next to Maxwell Harper, that is."

"Does Ethan know I'm with you?"

"He does now. He just spotted us."

She was happy to see Ethan coming

toward her. He looked great in the black denim jeans and black polo shirt he wore. The collar and sleeves of the casual shirt was trimmed in white. The closer he got to her, the more excited she became.

Ethan kissed Dakota softly on the mouth. "Hey, lady, fancy meeting you in here." His eyes encompassed Charlene. "Thanks for inviting me to lunch. I'm really happy you thought of it."

"I know. You've only had a huge grin on your face since you first spotted Dakota. Come on, guys. I'm starving. Ethan, you know what shopping does to me."

"Yeah, I'm afraid I do." He took Dakota's hand. "Seeing you here is a nice surprise for me. I hope this unexpected lunch date won't void our meeting tonight."

"Not unless you nix it. I've been thinking about it all morning." Dakota didn't anticipate her ever canceling a date with him, not the way she enjoyed his company. Seeing Ethan every day worked for her.

Dakota rushed into Danielle's room and gave her a huge hug. "How's my little snuggle bunny today?" Dakota asked excitedly.

"Okay. You look pretty," Danielle said softly.

"Thank you." Dakota sat down on the bed and kissed the child's forehead. "You look pretty cute yourself. Did you pick out your clothes this morning?"

"Yep. Nurse Compton helped me," Danielle said, her tone melodic.

Dakota pulled Danielle to an upright position. "That was nice of her. You're lucky to have a friend like her."

Grinning, Danielle nodded. "I know. Did you bring me something?"

Dakota gave an apologetic look. "No, not this time."

Danielle shrugged. "That's okay."

Dakota then pulled from her large purse a pink plastic bag and handed it to Danielle. "I told a fib. Here's a little something for my best girl."

With excitement written all over her face, the child reached into the bag and pulled out a cute red nightshirt. "Thank you. I like it." She reached out to Dakota for another hug. "I really like it."

"I'm glad. I know red is your favorite color. I bought a red dress for myself today so I thought I'd get you something in red, too."

Dakota looked around for more bags. "Where's your dress?"

"At home. I'll bring it up here for you to see."

"When?"

"Maybe after work one day this week."

"I can't wait," Danielle remarked, sounding appeased.

"Me neither. Want to go down to the recreation room for a while?"

"We can have tea." Danielle's eyes brightened.

Dakota clapped her hands. "That's always lots of fun for us."

The recreation room was stocked with a lot of toys and games, but Danielle's favorite thing to do was for them to pretend having tea using the children's tea set.

"Do you want to walk or ride in a wheelchair?"

"Walk. I feel good today."

"That's really nice to hear." Dakota beamed at Danielle. She loved her hair in thick Shirley Temple curls. It was a nice change from the usual braids and ponytails.

Seated at the children's yellow-and-blue table and chairs set, Dakota watched through loving eyes as Danielle went through the motion of preparing tea for two on the play stove. They'd done this countless times, but Dakota still got a big kick out of it. It was nice to play and act as silly and carefree as a child.

Danielle came over and set down on the table two teacups and two saucers. She then made sure the sugar container was in place. Her movements were like dance steps as she bounced and twisted her little body around. She had good motor skills.

Danielle finally carried the teapot over to the table. "Shall I pour the tea for you, my lady?"

"Yes, my lady, please do." Dakota giggled. She had taught Danielle that line and how to speak it with a British accent. Dakota's gurgling giggles had Danielle clapping her hands with enthusiasm and laughing cheerfully.

A blessing was said over the tea by Dakota. Then she and Danielle tipped their cups together, smiling at each other. They put the cups up to their mouth and sipped on the imaginary tea.

This child's play went on for the next twenty minutes. Then they did the mock cleanup. Danielle cleaned the cups, saucers and teapot and Dakota wiped off the table. There were times when they ate cookies from the little plates and drank milk or juice from the teacups, but the majority of their tea parties were pretend.

Dakota and Danielle then played with dolls. The older sister chose the one that had real hair to comb. Danielle liked to dress Barbie up in several flashy outfits.

Wondering how Danielle would react to Ethan, Dakota studied her sister with quiet contemplation. "How would you feel if I brought a visitor to see you?"

Danielle's eyebrows lifted. "Who, Kota?"

Dakota folded her hands and placed them on the table. "A friend of mine."

"What's your friend's name?" Danielle looked very curious. "Is it a boy or girl?"

Dakota chuckled lightly. "A boy."

Danielle stretched her neck. "A boy! Is he your boyfriend?"

Not ready to give out too much information, Dakota only smiled. "He's a real good friend. Would you like to meet him?"

Bobbing her head up and down, Danielle's broad smile gave away her answer. "Yeah. What's his name?"

Dakota grew a tad apprehensive. "Ethan," she said with reluctance. "I can't promise to bring him here, but I'll try. He's a very, very busy person."

"Busy like you?"

"Way busier than me, Danni. He's a college professor."

"Kota, I'd love to meet your friend."

■ ■ ■ ■

Dakota dropped down on the sofa the minute she walked into the living room. The bottom of her feet actually burned like fire from the long day of shopping and visiting with Danielle. She wasn't sure a good soak would do any good. The great thing about it was that she had everything she needed for the gala. The choker-style crystal necklace and matching earrings complemented both dresses she'd fallen in love with. It had been hard for her to leave the black gown behind.

Less than five hundred dollars had been spent, yet Dakota knew if she added up the true costs, her bills would've been way higher. Charlene had told her the shoes she'd bought retailed around two-hundred-plus dollars.

Leaping off the sofa, Dakota trudged down the hallway to take a hot bath and a long nap. She had left home a little after 10:00 a.m. and it was now close to 6:00 p.m. As soon as Charlene had dropped her off at home, she'd left to go visit Danielle.

Ethan wasn't due at Dakota's place until nine-thirty or ten. He had to attend a special meeting with his fraternity brothers.

According to him, the meetings usually lasted until the wee hours of the morning. Once the business affairs were settled and the meeting adjourned, the guys hung around and partied the night away. He wasn't hanging out with the guys tonight, he'd told her. Not when he had a pretty lady waiting for him.

Dakota lay across the bed, fully clothed. Ten o'clock had come and gone. The clock striking midnight was approximately ten minutes away. No word from Ethan had her terribly worried. It wasn't like him not to call and let her know something. Not once had he stood her up nor could she think of a single time he'd called to cancel a date.

The thought to call him fleetingly crossed her mind, but she decided it wasn't a good idea. She didn't want to make him the butt of any jokes. If he was still out with his boys, a call from her might embarrass him. Something unexpected had to have come up. Ethan wouldn't neglect to call her without good reason.

Dakota did a quick about-face on calling Ethan. There was no reason for her not to call him. It was okay to let him know she cared about him and she really didn't think he'd mind. As she dialed his cell, she thought about what she'd asked Danielle. Her sister was open to meeting Ethan and now she had to see if he was receptive to the same.

Dakota felt it was time for the two people she loved most to finally meet.

"Hey, I miss you, so I thought I'd call to let you know. I hope everything is okay. I can't wait to hear back from you," she said into the recorder. "I love you."

Instead of continuing to wait on Ethan, Dakota went into the bedroom and changed into her nightclothes. It was time to get some sleep, if that was even possible.

Dakota not answering the phone had Ethan concerned, but he'd just heard her message. The meeting had run a lot later than anticipated, but the moment it was adjourned he'd called to let her know he was on the way. When she didn't answer, he'd decided to hang out with the guys until he got a hold of her. She normally wasn't out this late, but maybe something important had taken her away from home, he considered.

With access to both a Ping-Pong and pool table, this group of grown, macho men acted like little children just to try to prove who the best man was. Everybody wanted to show off their skills and end up the winner. Ethan was used to joining in the fun and games with his frat brothers, but he had something else on his mind tonight. His thoughts were on something sweet, soft and someone deliciously feminine.

Maxwell offered to get Ethan a glass of wine, to which he declined. "What's going on? You've been acting odd ever since the meeting ended."

"It's nothing, man, I have to drive. I'm not trying to kill anybody."

"We'll just crash here at Rudy's place like we always do."

"That's not happening tonight. I promised to see Dakota after the meeting."

"Well, then, you'd better get going. What're you waiting on?"

Ethan shrugged. "Can't reach her."

Maxwell laughed heartily. "*You* can't reach your lady?" Howling, Maxwell put his hand on Ethan's forehead. "You sure you're feeling okay?"

Ethan playfully shoved away his friend's hand. "Get out of here with that crap. Something must've come up at the last minute."

"Something so important she wouldn't call and tell you about it?" Maxwell taunted his best friend.

"Give it a rest, man." Ethan ran his fingers

through his hair. "I'm out of here. It's late. I can't risk falling asleep at the wheel."

"You sure can't," Maxwell said knowingly. "I'm willing to bet that you're heading straight to Dakota's place. Whether you know it or not, you're in love with Miss Dakota Faraday."

Ethan nodded. "And you should've been there when that astounding revelation hit the dead center of your best friend's heart. It was powerful."

Maxwell shook his head. "I already know what it's like. Love *is* power. Charlene and I are inching closer and closer to I dos."

The two best friends shook hands on the promise of making contact with each other later in the day. Ethan quickly went through the house and said his farewells to the brothers still there. The group had gotten pretty lively, so he imagined this shindig wouldn't end much before the sun came up. If Ethan had his way, he and Dakota would share another amazing sunrise.

After scrolling through the names, Ethan stopped on Dakota's and hit OK. As he slipped under the steering wheel, he hoped she'd answer.

Dakota's sleep-filled voice on the other end of the line made Ethan smile. "Sorry for waking you up, but I had to call you and let you know what happened."

"Just knowing you're okay is all I need. I've been worried. I waited up for you until a little after midnight."

"This is my fault. Looks like I got my wires crossed, literally. I started calling you right after the meeting but didn't get an answer. I've been ringing your cell all this time, thinking it was the landline."

"I didn't hear my cell phone. I must not have charged it. But that's neither here nor there. I'm just glad to know you're fine."

"I feel the same way. I've been worried about you, too, thinking something might've happened. Now that we both know we're okay, I'll let you get back to sleep."

The silence from the other end came through loud and clear to Ethan. "I'm guessing it's probably too late to come see you now. Is it?"

Dakota's displeasure quickly turned to elation. "I'll leave that up to you, but I doubt I can get right back to sleep."

"I think a positive answer is hiding in there somewhere. I'll know for sure if you open the door when the bell rings."

"In that case, we'll both know," Dakota responded, laughing inwardly.

■ ■ ■ ■

Ethan pulled Dakota into his arms the moment she opened the door. "You have no idea how hard I prayed for you to let me in."

She smiled up at him. "Did you really think there was a chance that I wouldn't?"

"I'll never take you for granted." He held her at arm's length. "You look beautiful. I love the silk pajamas," he said, rubbing his hands up and down her arms. "Soft and silky, just like you."

Ethan slid his arm around Dakota's shoulders as they walked into her bedroom. "We can't make up for lost time, but we can sure try."

CHAPTER 12

As always, Ethan had a hard time keeping his eyes off Dakota. Totally transformed, angelic, beautiful, stunning, steaming hot and elegant were all the words running through his mind. Her hair looked sensational, full of body and bounce, swaying every time she moved. Never had he seen it looking shinier.

"Charlene took me to her salon," she said, sounding so proud.

"The stylist did a remarkable job. Your hair is beautiful."

"Thank you," she sang out, smiling brightly.

The red dress Dakota wore had him practically outright panting. But all the credit couldn't be given to the gown. Her body snugly fitted inside the material was what had him turned on. "You smell so good. Is it the perfume I gave you as a gift?"

"That it is! It's the perfect scent for me."

Nothing whatsoever could turn him off this evening. She always looked exceptionally nice, but he was completely enthralled with her exquisite appearance.

Dakota took another eyeful of Ethan. "I think you look dignified in black-tie attire. The tuxedo fits you beautifully and I love the cuff links' diamond sculptured *R,* representing your last name."

"Thank you." Ethan followed up his verbal gratitude with a staggering kiss.

Dakota's smile was sunny. His charisma had been working on her every single minute since he'd first arrived at her front door, bearing a beautiful corsage of baby's breath and red rosebuds. She was full of romantic expectations for the evening.

"Maxwell and Charlene are waiting in the limo. I had them meet me. I'm leaving my car here. We'd better go."

She picked up her evening bag from the coffee table. "I'm ready."

Charlene and Maxwell were also dressed elegantly for the special event. Dakota had gushed over Charlene's midnight-blue sequined gown the moment she got into the limousine. Maxwell's image mirrored Ethan's in a traditional black tuxedo.

Once the limousine pulled away from the curb, Ethan busied himself by pouring four glasses of white wine. "I'd like to make a toast to a fantastic evening. May the event be as special as it always is." Ethan tapped his glass against Dakota's before leaning in to give her a kiss.

Maxwell held up his glass and followed Ethan's lead. "Hear, hear," he said, tenderly kissing Charlene's mouth.

As the two couples walked around the California African-American Museum, viewing the items available to bid on at the silent auction, which was to continue throughout the evening, Dakota could barely contain her excitement.

Dakota continuously nudged Ethan, pointing out to him persons she easily recognized. "There are so many celebrities in this place . . . sports figures, actors."

"They come out in droves every year. This is a significant event for us. The museum can always use donations. The California African-American Museum's doors are kept open with support from the members and the community and their generosity," Ethan explained.

Dakota's eyes were wide as she looked over the auction items. "My goodness, Ethan, the typed index card says this boxing glove has Muhammad Ali's original signature penned on it."

"Amazing, huh? I can't wait to see your face later in the evening when you see Muhammad Ali in the flesh."

Ethan pointed at the original pastel and acrylic painting on paper. "This was painted by Bay Area artist Dewey Crumpler. It's also being auctioned. He's well-known for the Paul Robeson Collection."

"I've heard his name mentioned a time or two, but I don't know a lot about him. I'm going to make it my business to read up on Mr. Crumpler. Now that I've seen his work, I want to know his story."

"It's quite an interesting one," Ethan assured her.

Dakota's hands trembled when she reached out to touch the leather-bound copy of Senator Barack Obama's speech on race delivered in Philadelphia in March 2008, which had his original full signature.

"Another ongoing chapter of history is being written." She looked up at Ethan with longing. "If only I had the money to bid on it. I can't even imagine how much someone is willing to pay for that huge slice of history." Her hand still shook as she reached out and smoothed it over the soft leather.

"I wouldn't be a bit surprised by how much it'll go for. It's priceless. The one-week stay during any week in June on Martha's Vineyard will make a fabulous getaway, too. There are so many other fine works of black art available for bidding."

Ethan paused for a moment, listening intently to the address coming from the overhead speakers. "Dinner is about to be served." He cupped his hand under Dakota's elbow. "Let's get back to our table. Once dinner is over, the program hosts will follow up with an address to the attendees. Then the award presentation ceremony will begin."

Seated next to Dakota at the formally dressed table they shared with Maxwell and Charlene, Ethan found himself wanting to kiss Dakota every time he looked at her. He'd heard very little of what was going on around him. She looked that smashing.

Feeling a bad-boy mood coming on, Ethan leaned over and whispered something to her, kissing her gently behind her ear.

Dakota's color rose. "Behave yourself. We have a few hours to go yet," she whispered back. "But I know how you feel. I can't wait to *have* you devour me."

Winking, Ethan laughed softly.

Dakota's eyes danced flirtatiously. "And I already know what I want for dessert."

The room fell into a hush as the benediction was eloquently presented by a prominent African-American, Bishop Walter Cleary, the pastor of a mega-church and congregation in the heart of the inner city.

Formally dressed waiters and waitresses suddenly descended on the ballroom. Working very quickly, deliberately, they made the rounds, serving each of the guests the first course, a crisp garden salad and a mixture of piping hot rolls. Petite filet mignon, baked potatoes and asparagus had been chosen for the entrée. Cherries jubilee was the selected dessert.

"Look," Dakota said, "Dennis Haysbert is heading to the podium. Try to be nice now. I know you can do it," she teased, trying to keep him in line.

"Yes, I can." Ethan reached under the table and squeezed her thigh in response to her gentle chiding.

The actor's deep voice commanded everyone's immediate attention and the room grew pin-drop silent once again.

The silent auction and the time for dancing to a variety of music was again mentioned before the speaking portion of the program came to a close.

Thrilled by what she'd witnessed, Dakota clutched at Ethan's arm. "Thank you," she whispered. "This is a night that'll live on and on. It's very special."

Ethan knew Dakota had meant every word she'd said. He squeezed her hand. "You're welcome. I'm glad we could share this night together."

"I am, too." Dakota briefly thought about what a night like this one would mean to her parents and grandparents. She was sure they'd all be thrilled over it.

Ethan sensed the moment of sadness in Dakota. "Are you okay?"

"I'm fine. I was just thinking about my parents and grandparents and what they might think of this night."

He hugged her warmly. "I'm sure they'd be very proud, just as we all are."

Charlene got to her feet. "Interested in going to the ladies' room, Dakota?"

Dakota stood. "Excellent timing." She leaned down and kissed the top of Ethan's head. "See you in a minute."

Charlene politely excused herself to Maxwell and Ethan. She then slid her arm through Dakota's. "Having a good time?"

"A marvelous time! This is unbelievable."

Charlene couldn't help but feel Dakota's exuberance. She hugged her tight, as though some of the enthusiasm might rub off on her. "You're flying high, girl. I like your energy. It radiates." The shopping date had given her a lot of insight into the real Dakota.

The two ladies made minor repairs to their makeup before quickly returning to their handsome escorts. Both men stood as the women approached the table.

Charlene took Maxwell's hand. "We all know about being politically and socially correct, so we need to do a bit of mingling with other friends and colleagues. You are both welcome to come with us. If not, we'll catch you on the dance floor."

"Thanks for the invite," Ethan said, "but we're going to sit for a few minutes before we begin dancing away the rest of the evening."

Once the other couple left, Ethan turned his full attention back to Dakota, taking hold of her hand. "Your smile is as bright as the sun. I'd be willing to make a wager on your body being just as hot."

"I guess you'll have to wait and see." She flashed him another dazzling smile. "I'll tell you later which one I cast my vote for."

"Because I don't have a choice, I guess I'll have to wait. In the meantime, would you like a glass of wine?" Ethan asked.

"Yes, thank you."

"Any preference?"

"Please choose for me."

Ethan grinned. "I've already chosen something sweet and mellow for you. Me."

"Hmm, it sounds delicious. And I imagine it'll taste even better."

Ethan summoned one of the waiters to take his drink order.

By the time the waiter came back with the glasses of wine, the band had struck up the music. Both Ethan and Dakota took a sip of their white wine before heading out to the dance floor.

Ethan whirled Dakota all around, his eyes flirting with her all the while. The band was playing Chaka Khan's "Angel." "I like this song. You're my angel, you know. Loving you the way I do feels so good to my spirit."

She laid her head against his chest. "We're on the same page. I love you and I love the way you love me back."

The older crowd flocked to the dance floor when the band cued up Kool & The Gang's "Get Down on It."

After sitting down on the bed, Ethan took off his shoes. He then pulled Dakota onto his knee. "I need you," he whispered. "Badly."

Gently pushing his head back, she briefly

took liberty with his juicy lips. "The need is mutual. I can't believe how the evening flew by. I wish it could've lasted longer. Being out with you is so much fun. You sure know how to treat a lady."

He lifted her chin with his knuckles. "Only this lady," he said, massaging her heart with the point of his index finger. "You make treating you good easy."

"I was hoping I wouldn't embarrass you tonight. I'm not a worldly person."

Ethan smoothed her hair back. "You're my whole world and I want to be yours."

"Really?"

"Really. Girl, one day you're going to learn I'm a man of my word."

I hope so. There's a lot you don't know yet. Will you want me to be your world after learning about my sister and the job I do? "I just wanted to hear you say it again."

"You're my world and I want to be yours," Ethan reiterated for her.

She kissed him passionately. "You are. And you've been making mine go around until I'm dizzy in the head."

"Dizzy, huh? I like that. You keep me off kilter, too."

"I'll remember that," she purred softly in his ear.

Ethan stood up and unzipped Dakota's

dress, slipping it a quarter-way off her shoulders. His lips wandered over perfume-scented skin, tasting her sweet flesh. Continuing to slide the dress down her body, the material slowly fell away, exposing her breasts. He felt a sharp intake of breath. While closing his hand around her left breast, his mouth sought out the right nipple, suckling it gently.

Locking her hands together behind Ethan's head, Dakota enjoyed the pangs of pure pleasure coursing through her body. As he peeled off her dress completely, the electricity in his touch had her eagerly but foolishly wishing for forever in his arms.

Ethan was nearly tearing himself out of his clothing in desire. She stilled his hands, slowly removing his bow tie. After her fingers easily flicked open the buttons, she popped the suspenders before removing them to get him all the way out of the shirt. Undoing the top of his formal slacks in one swift motion, she unzipped the fly. Kneeling, she removed his briefs. Working her way down to his socks, she pulled them off, pressing kisses up and down his legs and inner thighs.

Ethan was half-crazed. Being inside her was the only way to relieve the blood pounding through his manhood like a raging river. Getting to his feet, he twisted his fingers in the corners of her bikini and hurriedly took them off. Backing her against the bedroom wall, he lifted her leg over his shoulder. His fingers tenderly entered her, readying her to receive all of him.

It was so easy for her to lose herself to the sexual thrills his hands and mouth provided. Ecstasy resided in his fingertips and his tongue. As his hands continued to tenderly manipulate her naked flesh, the mindless moans he made had her out of her head with longing.

Ethan's delightfully tormenting foreplay had Dakota crying out his name. Dying to have his body ravage hers, she curled her hand around his manhood, traveling up and down his shaft, slowly guiding him inside her.

As Ethan thrust upward into her femininity again and again, the moisture pooling inside of her had him propelling himself against her slightly forcefully, yet careful not to cause pain. She shuddered every time he tenderly stroked her inwardly. She loved it when their bodies united as one. The wall was cool to her back, which felt good against the heat of the out-of-control inferno.

"Now," she screamed out, "right now."

She felt herself floating into nothingness. Shudders rippled violently through her, pushing her past desire and over the edge of fulfillment. She knew they'd released at the same time. His rigidness filled her up and his body was trembling uncontrollably, causing him to gasp hard for air.

Falling down on the bed, he brought her in to lie with him, nestling his head between her breasts. "You leave me breathless every single time," he panted. "I love you more than you probably think."

Dakota hushed him with her lips. "I love you just as much," she murmured against his mouth.

Ethan awakened to find Dakota watching television, the volume turned down low. "What's the matter, sweetie? Can't you sleep?" He looked worried.

Dakota shook her head. "I've only been awake for a short while. I tried but I couldn't go back to sleep, so I decided to watch some of the programs I missed but taped with TiVo. Do you want me to use the headset?"

"That's not necessary. I'll watch the story with you. Sports, biographies and the history channel are what I get into when watching television."

"Some of the movies on cable get pretty crazy."

As soon as the story opened, Ethan immediately grew mum.

Several minutes into the movie made for cable, Dakota wished she hadn't turned on the television. If only she'd known what the story was about.

An hour later, the compelling ending had Dakota in tears. Stunned by her unexpected emotional outburst, Ethan wasn't sure what to say or do, so he just tenderly pulled her into his embrace.

When she turned in to him, burying her face against his chest, his arms tightened around her. "Calm down, Dakota. It's only a story. Don't let it upset you like this."

Lifting her head, she looked into his eyes. "It's much more than that. This story line is all too real, art imitating life, if you will. Millions of families have someone in their household living with Down syndrome."

"I'm not insensitive to this. I just made a stupid statement without thinking. Looks like I failed to calm you." The passion she felt had come through loud and clear in her comments, making him wonder if she knew someone affected by it. If so, he'd have to wait on her to enlighten him.

Dakota eyed him curiously, her eyes

glistening with unshed tears. "Do you think you could handle living with someone with Down?"

Ethan shrugged. "I don't know. I'm sure something like that is hard to deal with for a number of reasons. I don't know how families manage to make it through when a loved one isn't well. Life is hard enough as it is. Serious medical challenges can only add to the dilemma. My hat is off to the people who take care of someone sick. I'm not sure I could do it, but I'd never say I wouldn't try. We just don't know what we're capable of."

Dakota's optimism dimmed considerably, as if she hadn't heard his last remarks. "Maybe you really think families should just put their loved ones away in a facility, so they don't have to be bothered," she spat out, moving slightly away from him. "Perhaps locking our medically challenged away from the world, like they never even existed, is best for everyone concerned."

Ethan's stunned look turned to outrage. "Do you seriously think like that? If so, I feel sorry for you. I didn't say anything close to what you just said."

"You didn't have to, Ethan. Your eyes said it for you."

"Bull! I'm not claiming something that

never crossed my mind. I don't know how you came to that conclusion. You didn't get it from my lips or my eyes. That's a fact."

Dakota suddenly looked both regretful and sad. Finally, she cried out in silence. She had finally said aloud what she thought people were thinking about her. No one had accused her of putting Danielle away, but at times she felt like she'd done exactly that.

Guilt over Danielle's residential placement was the major crux of Dakota's anxieties and insecurities. Never mind the serious medical reasons that had prompted placement; Dakota often felt like she had deserted her sister, abandoning her when she'd needed her most. Guilt was the real archenemy. For sure, she'd been unfair to Ethan.

Why did she keep putting both feet in her mouth?

Dakota couldn't explain it, but if she kept up this negative behavior, she knew she'd end up choking herself to death or suffocating the relationship. It was best to get off this subject before she broke down again. She'd finally come face-to-face with what had kept her down. Now she had to find a way to rise back up to the top, for everyone's sake.

"Saying I'm sorry somehow seems inadequate, but nevertheless, I apologize. The story upset me and I take full responsibility for getting carried away emotionally."

Ethan drew Dakota back into his arms and kissed her forehead tenderly. "It's okay. Believe me, I understand." He *didn't* fully understand, but he couldn't tell her that for fear of her going off the deep end again.

Dakota shook her head in dismay. "I'm surprised you understand because I sure as hell don't. I can't believe I screwed up so badly again."

He smoothed back her hair, his fingers lingering against her skin. "No one screwed up. We just had an unfortunate misunderstanding. That's all there is to it. It's over now."

It'll never be over for Danielle, but she needs to be back home with me.

Dakota's mind reverted to Ethan's last remark. "It *is* over. I'll leave it at that. Is there anything you want to watch on television?"

"You can turn it off if you want. I just want us to concentrate on you and me."

She picked up the remote and flipped off the set.

Dakota tangled her fingers up in Ethan's hair, showering his face with soft kisses, hoping to forget her crazy meltdown. She was happy to have him in her life. The days they'd stay away from each other felt longer than normal. She had to do something different this time, had to figure out a way to meet Ethan's needs while making sure Danielle wasn't sacrificed in any way. She couldn't give up either of them and she hoped she didn't have to. She loved Danielle and was crazy in love with Ethan.

His uncertainty about caring for someone ill deeply concerned her, but she'd never know how he'd really react to her situation if she continued to keep the truth from him. She had to find the courage to tell him.

Ethan looked under the bathroom sink to see if Dakota kept any liquid soap there so he could shave. As he pushed aside a stack of brightly colored towels, a large photo album caught his eye. He wondered why it had been stored like this. He wiped off his hands with a paper towel and then picked up the album. Suddenly his breath caught. The Mongoloid features of the little girl in the oval picture on the front cover were distinct, yet she also resembled Dakota a lot. Inside were more pictures of the child.

Was the child in the picture Dakota's daughter? Dan's daughter, too, perhaps? If so, why hadn't she told him anything about her or him?

He studied the photo closely.

A ball of fire suddenly ignited in the pit of Ethan's belly. He was sure the little girl had Down syndrome, which would explain Dakota's reaction to the story line last evening. The emotion she'd displayed made sense now. What didn't make sense was why she had kept him in the dark.

Why couldn't she have told him she had a child, one who had health concerns?

As Ethan thought about his answers to the questions Dakota had asked him in reference to how he'd handle a loved one with Down, he knew he'd fallen short. His earlier words haunted him. Clearly, and in no uncertain terms, he'd let her know he didn't know if he could handle it. Had he been dead wrong when he'd said he wasn't insensitive? The things he'd said to Dakota had been terribly unfeeling, but he hadn't intended it that way. He *wasn't* an inconsiderate man.

How to let Dakota know she could trust him with anything and everything to do with her life was something Ethan knew he'd have to figure out — sooner rather than later.

In no mood to shave now, Ethan returned to the bedroom as a man with a totally different mind-set than from the one he'd had only minutes before. As he climbed back into bed with Dakota, he knew there were many fiery trials ahead of them. Getting her to trust him completely was the one he attached the most importance to.

While Ethan wouldn't just outright ask Dakota about the picture, he wanted this serious matter out in the open. This issue was something they had to discuss. He still didn't know if he was fully capable of taking care of a sick child, but he'd never said he wasn't willing to give it a try. If that were to occur, Dakota would be there to help steer him in the right direction, to help him cope with whatever serious challenges arose.

Apparently she'd been coping with this situation all alone. As much as he hated the thought of her having a baby with another man, he hoped the father was a responsible man. *If Dan was the father, was he involved with his child?*

Where did that leave them? Ethan had no choice but to wonder.

CHAPTER 13

Dakota still felt a little nervous about Ethan coming over this evening. Over the phone he'd mentioned they needed to have a serious talk. To bring or not to bring Danielle out in the open was no longer an option for her. That she and Ethan had confessed to loving each other meant something to her. Love involved trust and all her secrets had to be exposed.

Believing she was in love with an understanding man gave Dakota more courage than she'd otherwise have. She had to believe he'd give it his best shot once he found out about Danielle. That is, if he really loved her. If not, then that truth would also come to light. Either way, win or lose, tonight was the night for putting all the cards on the table.

What had she been thinking? She hadn't been thinking, she easily concluded.

Dakota grilled chicken and baked macaroni and cheese for dinner, but her appetite was lost. She saw Ethan eyeing her plate before he'd bowed his head to pass a blessing. All that was on her plate was a bowl with a small amount of salad in it.

Ethan raised an eyebrow. "Is that *all* you're eating for dinner?"

Her eyes narrowed at his cynical-sounding question. "Isn't it enough?"

Her response sparked the anger he carried deep inside. "Something tells me you have more on your plate, a lot more than what you've been willing to share."

Dakota laid down her fork and folded her hands atop the table. "Why don't you just come out and say what's on your mind? Something's obviously eating away at you." The frustration in her tone was apparent.

"Is that how you see it?"

"Ethan," she said sharply, "what are you getting at?"

"Your secrets, Dakota," he said plainly. "Why are you keeping secrets from me?"

"I'm sure that applies to both of us. We are *still* getting to know each other." She bit her nails.

"Maybe so, but you've said and done things that makes me think I don't know you at all. Sometimes you act like we're total strangers."

Ethan saw that Dakota was extremely nervous. Since he'd mentioned again that they needed to have a serious talk, she had been acting antsy. Biting her nails was just one sign of how on edge she was.

Pushing back from the table, Ethan created more space for himself and for her. "We've gone through a series of interesting changes since we first met. You know that as well as me. Are we on the same page so far?"

"I assume so," she said, failing to make direct eye contact with him.

"Let's start with your fear of commitment. You've been hurt and I understand that. It's a valid fear, but not a reason for keeping secrets and lying. Dakota, you haven't been very honest with me."

Her eyes blinked rapidly. "What . . . ?"

"You know the answer to that question, but I'll indulge you. I know I promised not to press you about commitment, but we've already gotten way past that. You said you were ready to commit and I believed you. Now there's one thing I'd like to know if you're so committed. Why didn't you tell me you had a daughter?"

Completely taken aback by his question, Dakota looked him dead in the eye. "I don't have a daughter. I don't have any children."

He didn't know why he believed her, but strangely enough he did. She hadn't so much as batted an eye. He had enough life experiences to know that people who lied couldn't control fluttering lashes. "Then who is the little girl in the photo album in your bathroom?"

Dakota closed her eyes for a brief moment. "She is my sister."

"Your sister?"

Dakota nodded, close to crying. "My sister, Danni, Danielle."

Ethan felt like he'd been struck by lightning. That the two different versions of the names were one and the same person shocked him and also made him feel stupid. Dan was not a man. She had a sister.

Ethan felt totally ashamed. "Forgive me. I thought . . . I need a moment to regroup."

Dakota looked like she was in pain. "My sister has Down syndrome. I planned to tell you this evening."

Not sure he believed the timing part of her statement, Ethan lifted his head and glared at Dakota. "Why this evening? Why not when we first met?"

"Just stop and think about how you're

reacting to it right now," she criticized, her voice high-pitched. "Maybe that'll give you the answer."

Stretching his neck, he stared hard at her. Her response was almost laughable, but this situation was too serious to make light of. The accusatory tone she'd taken with him wasn't sitting well. "Oh, no, I'm not letting you go there, lady. I'm reacting to what you haven't told me, not to what you said just now."

Tears formed in Dakota's eyes and she quickly whisked them away. She got up from the chair and walked over to the window, where she stood with her back to Ethan. The sinking feeling in the pit of her stomach made her nerves shriek. She had waited too long. He should've known the truth much sooner, long before he'd figured it out on his own. That only made matters much worse.

Ethan came up behind Dakota and rested his hands on her shoulders. "Don't shut me out. There's been enough of that already. I'm interested in hearing the truth."

Dakota faced him, looking right into his eyes. "You're right," she emoted, her heart trembling. "Let's go into the living room and sit down. There's a lot to say."

Ethan released his pent-up breath. Although he was glad everything would now come out, he wasn't happy with how he'd tackled it. Instead of saying something to show his regret, he took a hold of her hand and led her into the living room. He sat down on the sofa. She took a chair and turned it to face him.

Dakota wrung her hands together. "My parents died when a semi plowed into their car, killing them instantly." She paused for a moment to try to maintain composure. "Danielle and I went to live with our grand-parents. A short time later, they both died in the very same year, my grandfather pass-ing on first."

Dakota didn't even try to keep her raw emotions in check. She wasn't ashamed to show her humanity and to reveal to Ethan the devastations she'd been through.

His heart breaking for her, Ethan re-mained quiet.

Bringing her knuckles together, Dakota brought them up to her mouth for a quick moment. "I became sole guardian to Dan-ielle just as I turned twenty-one. While she has many of her own challenges to work through, she handles them with valor . . ." Dakota looked upward to heaven, silently asking God to help her get through these heart-wrenching revelations.

"Although her affliction with Down syndrome is considered mild, she has other issues, Down-related, that require skilled nursing care. Her heart beats erratically and it can pose a threat, affecting her ability to play, run and jump normally. She has respiratory problems, including frequent bouts of pneumonia. She was admitted to the Courageous Heart facility for around-the-clock care, after strong recommendations by her physicians."

The name of the facility was the same name Ethan had read from the building he'd followed Dakota to. *Did he tell her that?* If this was a session in honesty, he had to be as forthright as he wanted her to be. "I followed you to that facility the night you had the emergency. If you don't mind my asking, what was the emergency?"

Dakota was still stuck on his confession, wondering why he'd felt it necessary to follow her. "What made you do something as sinister as following me?"

"My confusion over the names. I thought you were seeing another man. I thought you were going to Dan and that he was the man you were once involved with."

She nearly laughed. "I'm sorry I gave you reason to distrust me. I know exactly where I went wrong. By keeping the truth from you I set the stage for what's happening between us. I guess what we both need to know is where we go from here. As for the emergency, it had to do with Danielle suffering an allergic reaction to seafood. To be more specific, the allergy is to iodine."

Ethan looked genuinely concerned. "Is Danielle okay?"

"She's fine. No more seafood or any use of iodine products." Dakota loved how gently Ethan had said her sister's name. She had been wrong about him for a long time and without good reason. He had just shown himself to be a man of deep compassion. His expression and intonation showed the same thing. He *was* concerned.

"You've been doing this alone for a long time. I commend you on the dedication. But it's not clear to me why you'd keep Danielle a secret. Please explain that."

Dakota ran shaky fingers through her hair. "Actually, it's unexplainable."

"Try."

Getting to her feet, Dakota began to pace the room, as she did when nervous. "Do you have any idea how some folks treat people who are frail?"

"I'm not some folks, Dakota. I've never given you any indication I'd mistreat anyone, let alone someone ill. I don't like the category you've stuck me in. And why in heaven's name would you go out with someone you had to hide a sibling from?"

Dakota walked over to the sofa and sat down. "You didn't deserve this. I've made a mess of everything. I'm sorry I used poor judgment. If you don't want to stay in this relationship, I'll understand. But I do love you. I know you're not the kind of person that I need to protect Danni from. I think I've known it from the beginning, but I failed to act on my intuition. I now realize I really didn't need to protect Danni that way. I created these protective mechanisms out of my own experiences with people who've hurt me."

Ethan put his arm around her shoulders. "I get what you've been through and I know you've sacrificed a great deal. But what I don't know is this. How can you say you love me and distrust me at the same time?"

"It was never a matter of distrust. I just didn't know how to tell you . . ."

"Because you didn't know for sure that I wouldn't hurt you. You put me right in the mix with all the others who've hurt and disappointed you. Don't hide behind your fears. They won't shelter you. Our relationship *can* be worked out, but we both have to be engaged in making it happen." With tears in his eyes, he tenderly captured her face between his two hands. "Do you really want us to work it out, Dakota?"

Tears spilled down her cheeks. "Of course I do. Are you saying you understand? Danielle is my flesh and blood. We're a packaged deal. I want you in my life, more than you know. I love you, Ethan."

He kissed her gently on the lips. "I'd never separate you from Danielle. Love is the most important element, yet we can't ignore what else is needed for us to succeed. I love you, too. Thinking you had another man nearly killed me. I misjudged you as well. I also showed lack of trust when I followed you and failed to bring the issues out in the open. I came here determined to do that. Now that we know what we're dealing with, let's take some time apart and think it all through."

"How much time?" Dakota asked, wishing her heart wasn't pounding so hard.

"As much time as we both need."

"Are you saying we shouldn't see each other?"

He looked aggravated. "We can't work this out by osmosis, but while things are fresh in our minds, we should take time to seriously consider every aspect of our situation. I don't want it to be over, but I need time alone to clear the cobwebs. But there's one more thing. I'd like to meet Danielle. Can we go there together?"

She was happy by his comments. "I'll put your name on the visitor's list. The nurses have to know who's coming and going on the floor for liability reasons."

Dakota didn't like the idea of their separating, yet she understood what he meant. She laid her head upon his shoulder. "We didn't finish eating dinner. Do you want me to wrap up something for you to take home?"

"That'd be nice." His appetite was gone, but she probably knew that. "I'll go back in the kitchen with you."

Ethan knew this was something both he and Dakota needed to be sure about. Neither of them had touched on anything to do with marriage. He wasn't sure if she had looked that far ahead, but he had mulled it over a time or two. He was in love with her. What he was sure about was not getting all wrapped up in Danielle's life if he and Dakota couldn't work out the stubborn kinks. He was the last person who'd want to subject this little girl to any kind of heartbreak.

At the front door, Ethan kissed Dakota. "I'll call you soon."

"Any idea when?"

"Soon." He didn't want to be tied down to an exact time frame. It could be today or tomorrow or next week. He just didn't know. However, he would call.

Dakota went into Ethan's arms, laying her head against his chest. "I'll be here waiting. Please don't forget about me. Take whatever time you need."

"Thank you for that. I promise to keep my word on calling." With that said, he walked away without a backward glance.

Ethan had had the last word, Dakota knew.

Seated at a desk in the back of the huge campus library, Ethan looked at the microfiche he'd been given to review at his request. Curious about the accident that had killed Dakota's parents, he wanted to read about what had actually happened on that tragic day. He saw it had made front-page headlines, but the actual story was printed on page eight of the A section of the *Los Angeles Times.* That in itself was a shame. He also had asked to peruse the *Herald Examiner* and the *Los Angeles Sentinel,* an African-American publication released weekly on Thursdays.

Line by line, Ethan scanned the newspaper article, paying close attention to every single detail. As he read on, his heart broke for Dakota and Danielle Faraday, two sisters who'd been orphaned. Their parents never had a chance to get out of harm's way and were killed instantly by the careening semi. Reading that the guy had no insurance coverage on a vehicle used for business had given him some idea of how much of an ordeal these past years had been for Dakota. The parents' life insurance money hadn't lasted very long. He was sure she'd done her best, but he wasn't so sure she knew it.

Inserting one of the other microfiche into the viewing projector, he repeated the same process, searching for the story on the Faraday accident. The details were practically identical, he noted. With the grandparents dying after the parents, according to what Dakota had told him, he understood why she hadn't enrolled in college until much later. Her wanting to become a special-education teacher made perfect sense to him right after she had told him about Danielle.

Ethan had presented himself to the on-duty floor nurse as a visitor for Danielle Faraday. "Dakota and I are close friends. I believe she put my name on the visitor's list."

Nurse Compton, who was standing behind the desk, heard the conversation. The nurses had been buzzing about Dakota informing them Danielle would have a male visitor, a friend of hers. Speculation was high.

Nurse Compton came up to the front counter. "I'll take this one, Sharon. I'm aware of this matter. Hello, sir. May I have your name so I can look it up?"

"Ethan Robinson."

"Thank you for refreshing my memory." Nurse Compton scanned the visitor's roster, looking near the end of the list, knowing it had been added only recently. "Here it is." She quickly reached for a visitor's badge and wrote down on it his and Danielle's last names and the room number. "Please put it on your shirt. It has to be visible at all times."

"Thank you, ma'am. I appreciate your help."

Outside Danielle's room, Ethan's head was bowed, as he said a quiet prayer. Since he and Dakota had talked about it a couple of days ago, he had decided to meet the little girl on his own. He wanted to get a real sense for how they'd do in each other's presence. He'd never been alone with a child in his life, but he had been around groups of kids on numerous occasions.

Ethan knocked on the door lightly and stood back to wait for a response.

"Come in," said a sweet-sounding little voice.

Hugging a huge stuffed animal under his arm, Ethan slipped into the room. "Hello, Danielle. My name is Ethan. Can I come in and sit with you for a while?"

Large eyes, full of guarded trust, swept over Ethan's face, then zeroed in on his cargo. She giggled. "Is that for me?" she asked, speaking over the sounds from the TV.

"It is."

"Why?"

"Because your sister told me what a special little girl you are."

"You know Kota, don't you?" She remembered Dakota calling Ethan's name.

"I do. We are good friends."

Danielle scrambled to sit upright in bed. "Kota's my sister and best friend," she said with pride, as if she had one up on him. "You can sit down."

Ethan brought the gray-and-pink pony over to the bed and handed it to Danielle. Dressed in jeans and a red sweatshirt, he thought she looked cute as a button. Her features spoke for themselves, but he saw no physical disability, nothing for anyone to bring to question. She resembled Dakota more in person than in the pictures.

Pulling the chair away from the desk, he stationed it next to the bed and sat down. "How're you feeling today?"

"Good. I *was* sick." She shook her head. "I can't eat seafood no more."

Ethan gave her a sympathetic look. "Sorry to hear that. I love seafood."

Danielle nodded. "Me, too." She shrugged it off, like it didn't bother her.

Ethan was discreet as he looked around the room to familiarize himself with the child's personal space. It appeared she had everything most kids probably had in their rooms. Dakota's mark was all over the decor. The areas were so colorful, warm and vibrant, a lot like her personality.

Ethan knew why Danielle had to stay in a private medical facility. He and Dakota had discussed it. Because of her erratic heartbeat she couldn't jump and run like other children and her respiratory system wasn't healthy either. She attended classes at the facility and interacted with the other resident children during playtime and special events. There were medical reasons for her to be placed there. Still, she looked very healthy.

"You play checkers?" Danielle asked, sounding hopeful.

Ethan nodded. "One of my favorite board games. Want to play a game or two?" Danielle's laughter was a trilling delight, making him feel warm all over.

"It's in there," she told him, pointing at a wooden cabinet with sliding glass doors.

While Ethan retrieved the checkerboard, Danielle slid out of bed and sat at the table. "I'm over here."

Ethan was surprised to see Danielle seated at the table. Her mobility made him happy. He carried the red-and-black box over to the table, where both players set up their side of the game board.

Ethan and Danielle enjoyed playing checkers together. He was surprised by how intently she studied the board. It was actually kind of cute. He loved it when she giggled and her laughter was infectious. The thought of allowing her to beat him only lasted a few minutes. She was good at the game and obviously played it on a regular basis. He guessed that Dakota had taught her and that the medical staff probably played with her, too. It would be easy to give in to anything Danielle wanted. Yet she didn't seem demanding, just very sweet, loving to be the center of attention. *What girl didn't?*

"Can you ring the nurse?" She pointed at the call button near the bed.

He grew concerned. "Are you okay?"

She nodded. "Just kind a thirsty."

"Can I have the honor of getting you something to drink?"

"I like orange soda. The nurse will get it if you ask."

"Okay. I can do that." Ethan jumped up from the table and went over and pressed the call button. It startled him when the nurse's voice came back at him over the intercom. "Danielle would like an orange soda. Can someone get that for her, please?"

"We will bring it in shortly. Can we get you anything, sir?"

"Thank you but not right now." He liked the nurse's cheerful voice, hoping the staff treated the little girl like a princess. Danielle certainly seemed to be happy living here. As he reclaimed his seat, he wondered what a place like this cost every month. Then he figured she probably received some type of medical benefits from Social Security.

By the time the nurse came into the room, Ethan and Danielle had finished their second game. He won the first and she took the last. She was a real trouper when it came to losing and winning. He was impressed that she didn't pout or gloat. Ethan noticed how polite she was to the nurse, thanking her for the soft drink, smiling sweetly.

"I'm sleepy," she told Ethan. She got up from the chair and went back to the bed.

He took that as his cue to leave. "Can I help you get back into bed?"

"I can do it." She had no problem climbing into her bed. "Can you come back sometime? Kota said you were nice."

Pleased that Dakota had mentioned him to Danielle, Ethan walked over to the bed and looked down at her. "You bet I can. What's your favorite cookie and chips?"

"Chocolate chips and Ruffles."

"I'd like to bring you some snacks the next time I visit. Is that okay?"

"Ask Kota if I can still eat it."

"I'll be sure to do that." Cookies and chips didn't have iodine in them, but he'd make it a point to find out if there were any other allergies. Ethan leaned over and kissed Danielle's forehead. "Thanks for the play date. See you soon."

"Bye," she said drowsily. With her eyes drooping, she wrapped her arms tightly round the pony, pulling it in closer to her body.

Ethan stood there in silence for a couple of minutes. His eyes swept the entire room for another look at where he'd been for the last hour and a half. He had just spent time having fun with the most adorable little girl he'd ever met. Dakota and Danielle loved each other. He had won Dakota's love, but could he win Danielle's love, too? He could hardly wait to try.

Persia was so happy to hear Luke's voice. She had had one hell of a horrific week and confiding in a friend was just what the doctor would order. "You couldn't have called at a more perfect time. This sister is feeling like crap."

"What's wrong? Is there something I can do to help?"

"I don't know." Persia chewed on her lower lip. All day long she had been contemplating meeting Luke in person. Despite company rules she needed a shoulder to cry on. A live body was needed in this instance. Not just a voice over the phone. "I'd like to meet you in person," she said, feeling like she had just bitten the bullet. If found out, she just might get a bullet right between the eyes. That's what being fired would feel like.

She would surely lose her job if her manager discovered she'd broken the rules.

"Are you sure about this, Persia?"

"No. But I want to do it anyway. Will you agree to meet with me as a favor?"

"When?"

"I'm off next weekend. What about early Saturday afternoon?"

That was nearly a week from now, but he was glad she hadn't asked to meet during the evening. That would've been hard to manage. "I think I can do it then, but can I call you back after I check my schedule?"

"Okay." She got the impression he was stalling for time. That was interesting because he'd suggested their meeting before she'd come up with the idea. "I'll wait for your call. Are you able to talk for a while?"

He chuckled. "You are too, too obvious. I called in to your line, didn't I?"

Dakota folded the last of her intimate apparel she'd taken out of the dryer. Leaving the small laundry room, she walked into her bedroom and put her items away in the drawers.

Feeling terribly lost, Dakota sat down on the bed and flipped on the television. For several minutes she surfed through the channels. Finding nothing interesting, she turned it off.

Her thoughts turned to Ethan, which was no big surprise. She missed him, but they both had done enough of that in the few months they'd been together. The holiday season was just around the corner. The thought of not spending them with him made her heartsick. If she wasn't at odds with him, he was upset at her. It had been nearly two weeks since she'd last seen him. It hurt like hell. Now she knew exactly what he'd gone through in her absence.

Would they ever be on the same page again?

The doorbell ringing startled Dakota. She looked at the clock. It was six-twenty Friday evening and she wasn't expecting a soul. Thinking it could possibly be Ethan, she jumped up and made a beeline for the front door.

Surprised to see Charlene standing there, Dakota opened the door. Charlene had only been there the day they'd gone shopping.

"Hi, Charlene," Dakota greeted cheerfully. "Please come in."

Charlene reached out to Dakota by giving her a warm hug. She then followed her hostess into the living room, where the ladies sat on opposite ends of the sofa.

Charlene crossed her legs. "Ethan told

Maxwell and me you and he were having a bit of difficulty. When I asked him if he minded if I dropped by to see you, he told me he thought it was okay."

"I'm a little surprised he didn't call to let me know about it."

"He wanted to but was afraid you might not agree to see me. He knows how folks can go into hibernation when relationships hit a speed bump. Ethan tells us you two are in love. In case you're wondering, we're thrilled. He also told us about little Danielle."

Dakota looked totally shocked. "He did? He's been busy, hasn't he?"

Charlene smiled. "Don't blame him. When we saw how down he's been, Max and I got up in his business, demanding he tell us what was wrong. Danielle is another reason why I came by. You are blessed to have her in your life."

"I've never thought differently," Dakota responded.

"I know you're aware that I work in special education. I'm in the company of children with Down syndrome five days a week and I volunteer at a special weekend camp so parents can get away for some me-and-we time. Still, I don't ever feel I do enough. I've donated a good chunk of my trust fund to families who can't pay the bills."

Grateful for Charlene's comforting remarks, even if she already knew how blessed she was to have Danielle, Dakota smiled. "This is a warm gesture on your part. I do appreciate it. And I'm sure you do more than your fair share. You don't have to volunteer but you choose to. You give your money when it's not required of you. God will reward you handsomely."

"He already does. Every single day I get to spend with my special-needs kids is rewarding." Charlene's eyes misted. "I know all about the sacrifices you've had to make, and not from Ethan. I just know from what I see every day."

"The sacrifices I've made have been worthwhile. I missed starting college right out of high school," she said, without sounding regretful. "Danielle needed me there full-time. Once the life insurance money ran out, I had to find a job. Food and drink was always there for us when we wanted it. All of a sudden I had to find a way to put food in the house and keep it in supply. I could no longer claim 'me time,' like you've mentioned. My time was no longer my own," she explained wistfully. "I was always too tired to read, a favorite pastime. I stopped trying to make friends because I couldn't attend social events when asked. Danielle comes first. That's how it'll always be."

Charlene's smile was sympathetic. "Sometimes people give up their dreams to help make others' dreams come true. That's what you've done. Know that you've done your very best. Take that well-deserved bow." She looked down at her watch. "The girls are getting together for dinner in about an hour. We'd love for you to join us."

The first thought through Dakota's head was to turn down Charlene's offer. But the sincerity in her eyes had her quickly rethinking it. "Maybe that's what I need to pull myself out of the doldrums. Where are you all dining?"

"Louie's Seafood Party at Marina Del Ray."

Dakota looked pained. "Do the others know what you know about my situation?"

"Absolutely not. We'd never discuss your private life with other friends. Our two guys are closer than some blood brothers. Ethan only told us because we pushed him hard and he needed sound advice. My credentials allowed him to make peace discussing it with me."

Dakota glanced at the clock. She had

showered, so it wouldn't take her long to get dressed and head on over there. "I know where it is. I'd love to come meet you guys."

"I came here hoping you'd go with me. Please let me do this for you. It'd be my pleasure. I've been where you and Ethan are, a few times, to be honest. You shouldn't be alone too often at a time like this. I hate being alone."

"Can you give me about ten to fifteen minutes to make myself presentable?"

"Not a problem. I can return Maxwell's call while I wait. He's been blowing up my phone for the past half hour. I couldn't answer because I forgot to hook up the hands-free headset before I drove off. The last thing I need is a ticket for yakking."

Both women laughed.

Promising not to take too long, Dakota quickly left the room. A warm feeling permeated her being as she made her way back to the bedroom. This was the second time Charlene had come through for her in a time of need.

CHAPTER 14

Finding himself standing at yet another front door unexpectedly made Ethan laugh. Just as Danielle didn't know she'd have him as company in her room a couple of weeks ago, neither did Dakota. He pressed the bell, hoping not to get into trouble for dropping in on her unannounced. It was important to tell her he'd seen Danielle because he'd thwarted the plan to do it together. Ethan hadn't expected a smooth first meeting, but he wasn't so foolish to think problems might not arise in the future.

Three additional rings proved futile. Ethan had to accept that Dakota wasn't in.

He turned around and walked back to his car, glancing at his watch. As he used the remote to unlock his door, a horn blew. Taking a look in the direction of the loud sound, he saw Charlene parking her car in the visitors' slot. He waved as he walked over.

Ethan sped around to the passenger side and opened the door for Dakota, kissing her softly on the cheek when she emerged. "I was about to leave."

"I'm glad I got here before you did. What's up?"

"Can we go inside and talk?"

"Sure." She turned back to Charlene, thanking her for a wonderful evening, asking her to call soon.

"I'll be in touch, Dakota. You can count on that. Good night." She gave the couple the thumbs-up sign before backing out of the slot.

Ethan and Dakota watched after the car until it turned the corner. He then looped his arm through hers, praying for a good visit.

Once inside, Dakota went back to the bedroom to put away her purse, leaving Ethan seated in the living room. Stepping into the bathroom, she washed and dried her face, freshened up her makeup and lip gloss and ran a few strokes of the brush through her hair. She was pleased to see Ethan, but she wondered why he was there. It didn't bother her, but it wasn't like him to drop by her place without calling.

Dakota sat in the chair facing the sofa where Ethan was seated. "You said you wanted to talk. I'm ready to hear you out."

Looking thoughtful, Ethan pursed his lips. "I met Danielle." He saw her eyebrows shoot straight up. "She's adorable. We had a good visit."

Dakota didn't look too happy about the news. "I thought we were going there together. What happened to make you go toss our plans?"

Prepared to answer her question, he clamped his hands together. "I had second thoughts about it and decided to meet her alone. I wanted it to be natural for both of us."

Dakota moved to the edge of her seat. "How did she react to you?"

"Once she found out I knew you, she opened up like a rosebud. Before then, she was reserved. She's a bright light. Danni asked if the stuffed toy I had was for her. When I said it was, she wanted to know why." Ethan went on to tell her the rest of the story.

Dakota laughed. Hearing Ethan tenderly referring to her sister as Danni was moving. "Sounds just like her. If she didn't like you, she wouldn't have asked you to sit down. Danni obviously trusted you. She's a good judge of character."

"I think so. Her beautiful eyes expressed

trust." He paused for a minute. "We discussed Danni's medical situation, but I'd like to know why you picked that particular facility."

"Because it's an extraordinary place for her to live. It's more like a home away from home. The staff loves her dearly and she loves them." She smiled as she thought of how well Danielle handled everything. "She can run out of gas pretty easily, but she's strong-willed. She won't ask anyone to do what she can do for herself. That child always has on her game face. I don't like her living away from me."

"Do you think she'll ever be able to come home to you?"

"It's my constant prayer."

Ethan carefully thought through the next topic of conversation. It was imperative that he was clearly understood. "We're in love, Dakota. Although we haven't touched on the subject of marriage we have to consider what's best for Danni. I don't want her and me to get attached, then have it end between us. That's no good for her. What I propose is to continue seeing Danni one-on-one. However, we'd also see her together from time to time. But she doesn't have to know we're romantically linked. Let her see us interact only as friends until our future is decided."

"You've really given this matter a lot of thought, haven't you?" She was impressed with his vision. That he didn't want to see her sister get hurt was heroic. "As friends or lovers, if she sees you regularly, she'll get attached."

He nodded. "It *has* occupied a lot of my time. I'm a deep thinker, not the type of person who just thinks about self. It's no longer just the two of us in this relationship. Three futures are involved. We've got our work cut out for us."

"What if things don't work for us?"

"I've thought of that, too." *God forbid that we don't work out.* "If that turns out to be the case, there's no reason I can't continue to be Danielle's friend. I can honestly commit to staying in her life. I'd like to meet the person who can keep from loving her. She has already stolen my heart."

Dakota was so pleased by Ethan's comments. He was an amazing person. *Why hadn't she trusted him with the truth from the beginning?* She already knew the answer, but she didn't like it.

Dakota got up and knelt down in front of Ethan. She took his hand. "Ethan, you've always proven yourself to be a kindhearted gentleman, but it took me a while to see you for who you really are, to see that you're a real man. I had to nearly lose you to realize that I'd already won your love. We can try it your way and see what happens. Danni will love having you as a friend. She'll be excited to have us both."

Leaning forward, Ethan sought out Dakota's lips, kissing her tenderly. He stroked her hair. "I'm happy we've come together to ensure that Danielle doesn't get hurt by our love affair. There are still a lot of things for us to figure out. We'll have to take it one day at a time to try to get it right."

We definitely have at least one extremely high hurdle to clear: my job.

Dakota sat in her car in the parking lot of the restaurant where she was to meet a friend. This wasn't the right thing to do, she knew. But she needed the advice of the man who'd become her confidant. Her world had been falling apart in front of her eyes when she'd first asked him to meet her. At that time, she'd had no one else to turn to. Everything had changed for the better and it was time to clear the last hurdle.

As hard as it was for Dakota to break company rules, she got out of her car and headed into the restaurant. This man only knew her as Persia, a sultry voice over the phone. But through need they'd come to discover they had something deeper in common. It was time for her to face reality. Ethan wanted to work things out and she wanted the same. She'd never be able to live with herself until he knew about her job. Perhaps with the proper advice and guidance she could get it right once and for all.

Ethan came through the front door of Miss Bee's, a family-style restaurant in Torrance, only to turn around and go back outside. He started toward his car, going back and forth several times before he finally went back into the restaurant. The place was crowded for a weekend afternoon. He began to look around for the woman he'd only seen in a television commercial, thinking she would be easy to spot.

Dakota suddenly looked up and saw Ethan stroll through the door. Immediately, she wondered why he was there. He couldn't possibly have known about her plans. Had he followed her again?

Still, she had needed to talk to someone since her future with the man she loved wasn't etched in granite, but it now had a chance to become permanent. Then there was the matter of what she did for a living that he knew nothing about. Despite her desire to tell all, she hadn't completely wiped the slate clean.

Dakota's eyes suddenly clashed with Ethan's from across the room. His eyes burned hotly into hers. Time stood still. That she was there to meet another man would hurt him deeply, especially because he desired to work things out. The meeting might be the final end-all. Truth, dare or consequences were facing her yet again.

Dakota stood and reached her hand out to him. "Ethan."

As though Ethan hadn't heard Dakota, he turned around and looked all around the restaurant again. He slowly turned back to her, hoping she didn't see how distracted he was. "What are you doing here? How is it we keep meeting in places we've never mentioned to each other?"

She knew he had referred to their meeting in the grocery store and at lunch with Maxwell and Charlene. They'd been estranged before the grocery store incident, only because she'd decided to distance herself from him. "Please sit down, Ethan. With me, there's always something I need to say. It's way past time for me to make a full disclosure."

Ethan pulled out a chair. "A full disclosure? I thought we'd done that already, Dakota."

"I'm here to meet another man."

Ethan narrowed his eyes. "What? Why?" His bewildered expression turned hard. "Does that mean I was right when I thought you were involved with another man?"

"I'm involved with many men. Not only have I cheated on you, I've cheated myself and Danielle. My deceased family would be ashamed of me. The man I'm meeting with is late, but even if he shows up he won't know what I look like."

"What are you saying?"

Dakota sighed. "You heard me right. He has no clue what I look like or who I am. He thinks I'm a hot, sexy woman in a television commercial. He's never seen me in person, like all the others. He's only heard the sultry voice I fake."

Her tears streamed. "I'm not in telemarketing, like I told you. I market sexual healing through conversation. I am a PSO, phone-sex operator. It's how I put myself through school and pay my rent and bills. It also helps pay the part of Danielle's residential care not covered by insurance."

Dakota's heart trembled. Oh, how he must loathe her, she thought.

"Would you mind repeating all of that?"

"I think you heard me."

"You're right, I did. Now let me share something with you." He paused. "I'm Luke Lockhart."

Eyes widening with disbelief, Dakota thought she was going into cardiac arrest. The pain striking her heart had rendered her immobile, otherwise she would've gotten up and run away by now. "I don't believe this." Her expression was one of utter confusion.

"Believe it. And you have a lot more explaining to do."

"I came to meet another man and you came to meet another woman. Is that what we're both doing here? You're Luke and I'm Persia." She laughed, but it came out terribly strained and unnatural. It really wasn't funny. Horribly painful was more like it. By the murderous look on Ethan's face, she thought he might be capable of killing her.

Wishing they both could be spared the pain of this crazy revelation, Ethan nodded. "I'm afraid so. I thought we had really talked everything through. But when it's put all together, it looks like we haven't said much of anything."

He suddenly leaped out of his seat. "I've got to get out of here. I know I can't deal with this rationally, not right now."

"No, Ethan," her voice thundered. "I need you to sit back down and listen." Her eyes pleaded with him. "Please."

Ethan sat back down. "Okay, Dakota Faraday."

"I didn't tell you and a lot of others about Danielle, but you're the only one who ever mattered. None of the reasons I made myself believe were valid. It had nothing to do with protecting her. I was protecting me. Overwhelming guilt kept me quiet, sheltering me from what people might think of me when they learned my baby sister was living in a medical facility. That I couldn't personally tend to her needs was more than I was able to bear. Big sisters are supposed to take control." Her tears began to drop like rain.

Ethan had already figured out what Dakota had just told him. He'd almost dared to tell her that the last time they'd talked. Then she had revealed similar things to him. Confronting her would've only added to the mountain of guilt she lived with every day. The good that might've come out of it was no match for the bad stuff she'd rather believe. Somehow, someway, he had believed she was destined to eventually figure it all out. He prayed morning, noon and night for the honest-to-goodness truth to be revealed.

Ethan covered Dakota's hand with his own. "You've got to give up the guilt. You have done everything humanly possible for that beautiful little girl. Your parents and grandparents have to be smiling down on you." He put his head down momentarily, trying to catch his speeding breath. "Please don't hate me for this, but I was able to locate old microfiche newspapers about the fatal accident. You've been beating up yourself for a very long time. Why can't you see all the great things you've accomplished?"

"Guilt. Something I've been living with for as far back as I can remember, way before Danielle was ever placed."

She lowered her lashes and then her head. The silence was dreadfully loud. When she looked up at Ethan, her eyes had refilled with tears.

Her hands gripped his thigh, squeezing tightly. "I even had the notion that if I'd been with my parents I could've somehow prevented their accident. There were a lot of *if onlys* in my life. Then came you, beautiful you, a man with the purest heart. The bright lights appeared in my life and the darkness lifted. You introduced me to things I'd only dreamed about. I assumed the life I lived was normal, especially when I didn't have anything to compare it to. As sure as I was breathing, I knew you'd also leave me one day. Now I know I didn't have anything at all to worry about. You have made all the difference in the world in my life. And I love you for it. I love you for you."

His heart was breaking for her. "You've somehow been able to rationalize all of this for years. Have you ever been to any kind of mental health professional?"

"There was no time or money for anything like that. School and helping my grand-parents with Danielle took up all my time. Then they died on me, too. Am I bad luck or what?"

"None of it has anything to do with luck, Dakota. You've got to believe that."

"I do believe it now, but look how long it's taken me. I couldn't come to terms with any of it. I mainly regret that Danielle had to suffer because of my guilt complex."

Ethan looked perplexed. "Suffer in what way?"

"Too many ways to count. Other than doctors and male nurses, she hasn't had any men in her life after her daddy and grandpa went away. And I swore off guys the last time I got my heart broken."

Her remarks reminded him of some of the

personal things Persia had told him. Since Persia and Dakota were one in the same, he saw the picture all too clear. "There was a lot of truth in some of the things you said, wasn't there?"

Dakota stifled a gasp. "Yes, the personal stuff." A lightbulb seemed to come on in her eyes. "It seems that there was duplicity on both our parts. You're no more an adult film star than I am a millionaire. You're a brilliant professor."

"Nothing I said about me was true except the part about liking you, about wanting to be your friend," he said wistfully. "If we didn't know who was on the end of the phone line, it looks as if our hearts undoubtedly knew."

Dakota loved the sound of that. "I believe our hearts did know."

"You had adopted a Southern accent and I had altered my voice because I feared some of my students might work there. When you think about it, this crazy story of ours is kind of remarkable. I'm writing my book on the adult entertainment industry and you provided me with a good bit of the information I needed. I can't believe we disguised our voices so well, even after we became relaxed in our conversations with each other."

Ethan wanted to laugh, but he felt too much like crying.

Dakota as a PSO was unsettling for him. *Was he a hypocrite?* He had called the sex lines, even if it was for his project, but he had to admit he'd come to care about the person he'd known as Persia. She had befriended Luke in return in troubled times. The lies Ethan had made up were obviously to protect his anonymity and to get valuable information, but nonetheless they were lies.

How did he accuse her of something he was involved in, no matter the reasons?

The amazing thing about all of it was that he and Dakota's souls and hearts had connected twice, wittingly and unwittingly. *Destiny?* "Who would ever believe us if we shared our story? People would swear we'd lost our minds."

Dakota looked embarrassed. "No one *but* us would believe it. And that's only because we've lived and breathed life into our alter egos. I didn't know any other way. If you'd see the size of my monthly bills I think you'd at least try to understand."

"It's not for me to understand. This is your life. Honestly. And you're right. There is no Persia King and Luke Lockhart. Our cover is blown to smithereens. But there is a Dakota Faraday and an Ethan Robinson.

What are we going to do about them?"

Ethan Robinson was the only man in the whole wide world for Dakota Faraday. While she'd been stupid enough to believe they could have it all, deep down inside she knew her lies would one day rip them apart. She'd completely blown what they'd had by keeping secrets and telling tall, ugly tales. She probably didn't have an ounce of credibility left with him. He had accepted Danielle, but she couldn't imagine him overcoming what she did for a living.

"I can't imagine any college professor who would have much to do with a phone-sex operator, other than use her to help him write a book."

Ethan pulled Dakota into his arms. "Sweetheart, no matter what we've done or said in the past, deep down in my heart I still believe destiny is calling. Tell me, do we heed the call or continue ignoring the love that's so profound between us? I love you, Dakota. The kind of love I feel for you is the forever kind. If I truly love you, I'll understand you did what you thought you had to. Your job shouldn't matter, but I'll have a hard time with it every time you leave for work. I'd go bananas if you continue working there. I want you to talk sexy only to me."

Unable to believe her ears, Dakota put some space in between them, looking up into his face. "Are you saying what I think you are?"

"Yes, Dakota, I am. I want you. I've wanted you from day one. I just need to know you want me, too."

"Oh, yes, Ethan. I do want you." She bit down on her lower lip. "I'm close to graduation and I'll get another type job until then. Destiny *is* calling." She'd said that like she finally believed it. "I'm not going to ask how you can love me after all this 'cause I'm just so glad you still do. Ethan, pinch me. I have to know I'm not dreaming."

"I'll kiss you instead. I want you to feel the passion." To show her he meant business, he kissed her thoroughly. "No more pain for you. Maybe we can continue being Persia and Luke if we have a need to spice things up," he teased.

"I doubt we'll need to do that. We're already pretty spicy in the bedroom."

"You are right about that. I love you and you love me. We've got it all."

Danielle was asleep when Dakota and Ethan entered her room. Instead of waking her, they sat at the table, staring into each other's eyes. A lot had happened in the past week, but even more had been resolved. They'd both made mistakes in this relationship, but not a single one was irreparable, not as far as Ethan was concerned.

"What do you say to looking at rings after we leave here?"

Dakota's eyes widened. "Rings? What kind of rings?" She held her breath.

"Engagement rings."

One eyebrow angled. "Are you getting engaged?"

"I'd sure like to."

"Who's the lucky lady?"

"I guess we'll have to wait to get her answer before I can say."

"Have you asked her?"

"No."

Hunching her shoulders, she turned up both her hands. "Why not?"

"There's an important third party to consult with."

Dakota frowned. "A third party?"

Ethan's eyes swept over the sleeping Danielle. "My future daughter."

"Daughter? What are you talking about?" Then her eyes followed his gaze. Tears sprang to her eyes at the same time his meaning sank in.

"I'd hoped it'd be obvious by now. If Danielle will allow me to marry her sister, then we can adopt her. I want that, Dakota. I'm even thinking of buying a new house because we'll need more space. Danielle belongs with us. She needs two parents. I want us to adopt her. Can I possibly get your answer before I get Danielle's? If you don't agree, there's no need to ask her. Will you marry me and let me be a marvelous husband to you and a loving father?"

"Yes, yes, yes." Running around the table to get to Ethan, Dakota screamed so loud that she woke Danielle, who shot straight up in the bed.

Ethan and Dakota rushed over to the bedside. "Hi, sweetheart. How are you?" Ethan asked Danielle, smiling down at her.

Danielle smiled brightly, her eyes on Ethan. "You *did* come back. I'm happy."

Ethan kissed the back of her hand. "Me, too, Danni." He leaned over the bed. "I have something important to ask you."

"What?"

"I'd like Kota to marry me and come live at my house. Will you please give Kota away to me?"

Danielle didn't understand and she began to cry. "Don't take Kota away," she sobbed, reaching out for her sister.

"No, no, sweetheart," he soothed, smoothing her hair. "I want to marry your sister and I want you to be a part of our lives and our wedding. We want to be together with you always, the three of us. And when the doctors tell us it's okay, we want you to come home and live with us. What do you think?"

Dakota grinned. "I like you more." She looked at her sister. "Kota, I love you. I can give you away if you stay."

Tears ran from Dakota's eyes. "Always, Danielle, you and I are forever. Ethan and I will always be here for you. We'll be one big happy family. I promise."

Ethan gathered Danielle and Dakota in his arms, hugging each of them tightly. "I love you both so much. Listen closely as destiny calls."

ABOUT THE AUTHOR

Linda Hudson-Smith was born in Canonsburg, Pennsylvania, and raised in Washington, D.C. She furthered her education at Duff's Business Institute in Pittsburgh. The mother of two sons, Linda shares a residence with her husband, Rudy, in League City, Texas.

In 2000, after illness forced her to leave a successful marketing and public relations career, Linda turned to writing for healing and as a creative outlet. Dedicated to inspiring readers to overcome adversity against all odds, she has published twenty-four acclaimed novels.

For the past seven years Linda has served as the national spokesperson for the Lupus Foundation of America. She travels around the country delivering inspirational messages of hope. In 2002, her Lupus Awareness campaign was a major part of her book tour to Germany, where she visited numerous military bases. Linda was also recently awarded the key to the city by the mayor of Crestview, Florida, for the contributions she's made by educating others about Lupus. Linda is an active supporter of the NAACP and the American Cancer Society. She is also a member of Romance Writers of America and the Black Writers Alliance.

To find out more about Linda Hudson-Smith, please visit her Web site at www.lindahudsonsmith.com.